Praise for *Losing It*

"Wise and witty . . . *Losing It* is cringingly insightful [about sex and] the ways we tie ourselves into knots over both. . . . [Rathbone's writing] sparkles with sharp images and painfully funny observations. . . . [She knows] what it feels like to be a smart, overly self-conscious young [woman, and] knows how crazy self-conscious women can seem. Rathbone [slyly] constructs a female protagonist who is a product of a sex-crazed culture but not a victim of it. . . . The genius of *Losing It* is that Rathbone resists turning her novel into a conventional romance."

—*The New York Times Book Review*

"A charming, truthful story about a lovably imperfect young woman whose virginity has overstayed its welcome; a witty and insightful novel about the mysteries of human connection."

—Maggie Shipstead, author of *Seating Arrangements* and *Astonish Me*

"Delightful . . . Sweet, funny and unexpectedly poignant, the book is *Bridget Jones's Diary* for the millennial generation." —*People*

"The mysteries of intimacy deepen in this mordant novel about taking charge and letting go." —*O, The Oprah Magazine*

"*Losing It* presents an accurate—and entertaining—depiction of what it feels like to be alive, right now, in this absurd, contemporary moment. Rathbone's accuracy is what makes her so funny; it's her grace as a writer that elevates this book from a series of comedic one-liners to art. . . . Emma Rathbone's project, it turns out, is more ambitious than expected. That's something to celebrate."

—Edan Lepucki, *San Francisco Chronicle*

"Like *The 40-Year-Old Virgin* for women . . . There's something unusually keen about Julia's observations, both those she makes of herself and those she makes of other people, with a colorful, razor-sharp specificity born of way too much time and energy spent watching life happen to other people." —*Vogue.com*

"It's part *Sisterhood of the Traveling Pants*, part *American Pie*, with a dry humor that'll keep you flipping." —*The Skimm*

"Julia's crises in life and love are cringeworthy in the best possible way, and Rathbone's hilarious novel will leave you begging for more." —*Glamour*

"Julia's desperation is tragic, hilariously funny, and all too relatable to anyone who has felt like life has moved on without her." —*Real Simple*

"[Rathbone] knows how to find the comedy in Julia's neurotic obsessive fantasies, and the tragedy in her series of unendingly terrible adventures in online dating. . . . She creates a different kind of story: one of neurotic self-obsession; of a smart, frustrated woman; of the unfortunate truth that so many women are convinced that their value depends on men's judgment—all within a narrative that actually has very little to do with men. It's a story that's [worth reading]." —*Vox*

"Rathbone's debut is whip-smart and wonderfully funny—if you're going to add one book to the list this month, let it be this one." —Refinery29

"A summer odyssey filled with awkward false starts and, hopefully, a happy ending." —Cosmopolitan

"A candid yet funny take on just what desire and love mean." —The Millions

"Losing It sheds light on alternative sex positivity (one that respects one's choice to wait), and shatters the stigma surrounding the subject, but not without plenty of humor involved." —Nylon

"Funny and insightful . . . Rathbone writes with pinpointed accuracy the feelings of discontent and despair that can arise from feeling lost or stuck in life. . . . [She] imbues Julia with such warmth and humor, and writes her with such affection, you can't help but root for the misguided character even when you want to shake her. This is a testament to Rathbone's writing and Julia's voice. . . . Losing It is a terrific and funny meditation on the deep pockets of discontent in life, growing up, and seizing the right opportunities for connection when you can." —The Rumpus

"A slightly neurotic and wholly hilarious meditation on the difference between love and lust, The One and close enough, Losing It is about so much more than a quest for sex: It's a confrontational narrative about all the other stuff that goes along with it, and the intimate decisions we make that shape our lives for better—and worse." —Refinery29

"Witty." —Us Weekly

"Every single page of Emma Rathbone's Losing It contains a line so funny, so awkward, so perfect, that you do not want this momentous summer to end. Rathbone's writing feels effortless, but it detonates in such wonderful ways. An amazing book." —Kevin Wilson, author of The Family Fang

"Emma Rathbone has the wisdom to understand that we are all the protagonists of our own stories, and the sense of humor to recognize the absurdity of that fact. With a delicate touch, Rathbone takes a fraught moment in one young woman's life and fashions a funny, sad, genuinely moving story from it. Her Julia Greenfield is entirely imperfect and completely sympathetic, and Losing It is a bright gem of a novel." —Lauren Fox, author of Days of Awe and Friends Like Us

"Wry and moving, a story about a young woman scuttled in love and work who fears that some kinds of loneliness might be impenetrable. A heartfelt and incredibly funny novel." —Thomas Pierce, author of Hall of Small Mammals

"A contributor to the New Yorker's 'Shouts and Murmurs' humor column, Rathbone reliably wrings the humor out of this situation, but more impressively, she manages to evoke its poignancy. . . . A̶̶̶ smart about people and unexpectedly sweet." —Kirkus Reviews

ALSO BY EMMA RATHBONE

The Patterns of Paper Monsters

Losing It

Emma Rathbone

RIVERHEAD BOOKS

New York

RIVERHEAD BOOKS
An imprint of Penguin Random House LLC
375 Hudson Street
New York, New York 10014

Copyright © 2016 by Emma Rathbone

The Library of Congress has catalogued the Riverhead hardcover edition as follows:

Names: Rathbone, Emma, author.
Title: Losing it / Emma Rathbone.
Description: New York : Riverhead Books, 2016.
Identifiers: LCCN 2016003534 | ISBN 9781594634772 (hardback)
Subjects: | BISAC: FICTION / Contemporary Women. | FICTION / Humorous. |
FICTION / Coming of Age. | GSAFD: Bildungsromans. | Humorous fiction.
Classification: LCC PS3618.A84 L67 2016 | DDC 813/.6—dc23
LC record available at http://lccn.loc.gov/2016003534
p.   cm.

First Riverhead hardcover edition: July 2016
First Riverhead trade paperback edition: July 2017
Riverhead trade paperback ISBN: 9781594634789

Printed in the United States of America
1   3   5   7   9   10   8   6   4   2

Book design by Lauren Kolm

For Adam

This is the heat that seeks the flaw in everything
and loves the flaw.
Nothing is heavier than its spirit,
nothing more landlocked than the body within it.

—Jorie Graham, "Tennessee June"

Losing It

— *One* —

I sat at my desk and stared at a calendar with a bunch of dancing tamales on it and played with a little piece of paper and thought about the fact that I was twenty-six and still a virgin. There was that, and then there was the fact that I couldn't stop thinking about it.

Chelsea Maitland. She was my first friend to lose her virginity. She was fifteen. She told me about it one afternoon on her parents' remodeled back deck after school. The railings were made of a bright white vinyl material that hurt my eyes. It was when she'd gone to visit her sister at college, she said. They'd gone to a frat party, and there was a guy there who had been a counselor at a summer camp she'd gone to. She'd always had a crush on him, and they ended up getting drunk and walking to a lake together and one thing led to another.

"How did it feel?" I asked. I focused on a laid-back ceramic frog with an outdoor thermometer in it. We lived in San Antonio, that's where I grew up, and fixtures like this were common. "I couldn't say," said Chelsea, with a little smile, her face folded and smug, like she was in possession of a secret I couldn't possibly fathom, and she had to crowd around it and protect it. Chelsea Maitland of all people. We'd been friends for almost eight years, since we were kids, but the implication beneath our friendship had always been that *I* was the special one. That I would always be the one to get the thing.

The phone on my desk rang. It was my boss.

"Hi, Julia," she said. "Can you meet me for a quick chat? Sorry, are you in the middle of anything?"

"Oh, no, no," I said. And then, before I could stop myself, "I was just staring at a calendar with tamales on it. That someone left here. I think. It's not mine."

There was a pause. "See you in ten?"

"Sure!" I said.

I shoved the calendar into a drawer and brushed off my desk and picked up and stared into my pen jar and put it back and just kept sitting there like that.

Then there was Heidi Beasley. We all found out at a sleepover when we were sixteen, on a rare weekend I wasn't away at a swim meet, that she had lost her virginity. What was it about her? I thought later, curled in my sleeping bag, staring at a wooden sign that read "Heidi's Bistro" in their finished basement. I'd known her forever, too. I remembered one afternoon in the activity room of a church—this was when my parents were going through their Christian phase—she'd cried because she was trying to thread a bunch of jelly beans into a necklace and they'd all fallen apart. And now her face was always soft with daydreams and she would thoughtfully chew the end of a lock of hair and stare into the distance. I'm sixteen, I thought at the time. It wouldn't be long before it was my turn.

I swiveled around and looked outside. I was on the twelfth floor of a glass building in a new development called Weston Corner in a nondescript suburb of Washington, D.C. I had a view of the plaza below where there was a fountain surrounded by large concrete planters, all deserted now because it was raining. A sandwich board fell over in the wind. In the distance was a half-completed hotel, and then beyond that, fields, nothing.

Danielle Crenshaw. She was on my high-school swim team and so we were at a lot of meets together. One afternoon we're all lingering, taking longer than usual. She's in purple leggings and a big floppy sweater and she's doing her favorite thing, which is to show off her sex moves via a little hip-hop dance. "Ya gotta get down on it," she said, rolling her chest forward and squatting. "Ya gotta get down on it." Everybody shrieked with laughter, including me, but really I was marveling at her authority with the subject matter. To have gotten down on it so many times that you could confidently riff on it like that without being afraid anyone would doubt your experience.

"Julia, I'm glad you stopped by," said my boss, Jodie. Her blond hair was pulled back into a burst of curls. Her desk was covered with papers and envelopes. She slammed her palm down as if they were all going to slide to the floor.

"Yup," I said, sitting down across from her. "Well, you asked me to." She shot me a look so I said, quickly, "I like it," and pointed at a decorative chunk of quartz on her desk.

She rolled her eyes. "Not my idea. But thanks."

Her phone rang. "Hold on," she said, and answered it. Sometimes Jodie could seem so distracted it was like all her features were swimming away from one another. I stared at a lipstick-stained coffee mug. "Quartz Consulting," it read in a casual handwriting font.

She put down the phone, laced her fingers together, and leaned forward. "The reason I asked you here—have you looked at *Education Today* lately?"

"Ha," I said. "Yeah." I thought she was joking. *Education Today* was the company's blog, and it was my whole job to run it and update it. I was supposed to comb the Internet for articles on higher education and trends in online courses, and then re-post them with the author's permission.

"I'm serious," she said. "Have you looked at it? Like a casual viewer?"

"Yes." I shifted in my seat. "Definitely, sure."

"Because on Monday you posted an article extolling the benefits of one of our main competitors."

"Oh my gosh!" I said, as if we were gossiping.

Her smile hardened.

"And I noticed the posts have been lagging," she said. "You've only put up two things this week."

"That's right." I cleared my throat. "It's been sort of a slow week in education news, so I thought I'd kind of see what happened and catch up towards the end."

"I guess I'm just wondering if there's anything you need to work at a slightly faster clip."

"Sure, yeah," I said, nodding quickly. "No, I'm fine. Just a little behind."

She leaned forward and rested her head on her palm and squinted at me. She smiled a searching smile.

I smiled, too, and raised my eyebrows, and recrossed my legs.

She stayed like that and held the silence and I was right about to point to a small decorative watering can on her desk when she finally said, "One more thing."

"Sure!"

"How's the Yacoma spreadsheet coming along?"

"It's getting there," I said.

"You must be, what, halfway through?" she said. "Three-quarters?"

"Yes," I said.

The Yacoma spreadsheet was a mountainous data-entry project where I had to enter payment information for every one of our hundreds of authors, going back six years. I'd barely started it.

"Great," she said. "Because Chris is going to be needing that pretty soon for the audit."

"Right, of course," I said.

"Glad you're on it," she said.

"Yup," I said. "I am."

"Good."

Back at my desk I sat down and looked around. Everything had a matte gleam—my chair, my computer, the door, the desk, the building itself. Someone's ringtone went off down the hall.

Senior year, there was Kimmy Fitzgerald. People liked Kimmy because she was nice to everyone. She always wore a winter coat that she allowed her grandmother to sew little bits of fabric onto, so that it made a kind of hideous patchwork, and she somehow got away with this due to a grave, dreamy manner that repelled criticism because you could tell on some innate level that she wouldn't care what anyone said.

One night a group of us girls were at an all-night Greek diner that people from our high school often went to. We were talking and picking at waffles and drinking coffee. At the booth next to us was a group of boys from another school being loud and stealing looks at us. We made a show of ignoring them. One was wearing a boxy black button-down shirt, like a waiter would wear, and had greasy blond hair, and a broad face with wire glasses that were too small. On first glance he looked pinched and insolent, like a bully. But then when we were leaving the diner, out in the parking lot, this same guy came up to us. His friends were hanging back, embarrassed, as he got down on one knee and presented to Kimmy a flower he'd made out of the paper place mat. "A rose for a rose, m'lady?" he said.

We all laughed in a mean, choppy way and rolled our eyes,

although you could see—in that gesture, where he was putting everything to the front, you could see the way he was brave and openhearted, even though he wasn't handsome or wearing the right clothes. Any one of us would have ignored him, but Kimmy didn't. She saw the happiness that was leaping out at her, and she took it. She stepped forward and, to everyone's surprise, said, "Why, thank you."

They started seeing each other, and sleeping together pretty soon after that. He came to the science fair at our high school and they both sat in front of her project, which was a display of little bits of charred carpet. They drew doodles and played with a calculator and laughed. He became more handsome, like you could see the best version of him because of her.

I opened a drawer and took out a pencil and started scribbling on a Post-it note, trying to see how dark I could make it. Jessica Seever came in and poured herself into the chair across from me. She worked at the front desk and was my only friend at the office. "Crazy night," she said, referring to the previous evening. We'd gone to a bar together and sat in uncomfortable silence until her new boyfriend showed up. Then they'd had a theatrical fight that they both seemed to enjoy.

"Kidman *does* like you," she said. Kidman was her boyfriend.

"Okay," I said nonchalantly, "sure." I opened a folder on my computer, suddenly finding, with Jessica's presence, the will to work on the spreadsheet.

"I'm actually—" I pointed at the screen with my pencil.

"Things just got a little out of hand," she said, proud of herself.

"Uh-huh."

"Look, it was me." She put her hand on her chest. "I started it. I always do! It's like Kidman says, I get some tequila in me, I go crazy."

"Right," I said.

"He's like, 'You're crazy, girl!'"

The first time we'd met, Kidman had barely acknowledged me, and then spent the whole night flirting with Jessica and looking around like he was really restless. Jessica and I were friends due to the fact that we were both unmarried and roughly the same age and had immediately established a mutual dislike of squirt-out hand sanitizer, which had not, in the end, reaped the conversational dividends I had hoped for. We spent a lot of time together poking at our drinks with our straws. She liked to say things and then gauge my reaction for approval or admiration.

"You know what they say," she said, tracing the arm of her chair. "Make-up sex is the best."

Her eyes roamed over my face. "Totally," I said.

"After you left we went out to his friend's apartment complex—have you ever done it in a pool?"

"Yes," I said. "A bunch of times."

In about four hours I would go back home to my apartment, microwave a dinner that would burn the top of my mouth, then float facedown on the Internet for a while before going to bed even though I wasn't tired.

"We were, like, up against one of those, like, floating things, with the tube? It was shaped like a turtle?"

"A pool cleaner?" I said.

"I guess. But he was behind me, and I was holding on to a ledge. We were in that position? And it kept bumping into his back and he was like, 'Get it away!' and I was like, 'Threesome!' And he was like, 'You are so bad.'"

"Yikes," I said to Jessica, trying to muster the same wry glint in my eyes.

At the science fair, Kimmy and Jason had touched each other with total ownership, like it was just a given that they had access to each other all the time. At one point I saw him lift her hand and place it in his palm and study it like it was a precious jewel. I'd never had anything like that. I'd graduated from high school, gone to college, graduated, gotten my first job, and I'd still never had anything like that. Not even close.

"So good," said Jessica. "So hot." She looked at me for a reaction.

I swiveled around and stared at the empty town center. Sometimes, thinking about those two—Kimmy and Jason—I felt a sense of loss in my own life so drastic it was like the wind was knocked out of me.

"You want to come out tonight?" said Jessica. "We're going to this new place."

"No," I said quietly. I turned back around. It's funny how a decision you've been making in difficult increments can suddenly seem like the simplest thing in the world. "I'm leaving."

"What?" She looked at me, perhaps for the first time, with genuine interest.

"I'm quitting," I said. "I'm quitting this afternoon."

"You are?"

"Yes."

"Awwww," she said, staring at her fingernails, a million miles away.

It hadn't always been like this. Before I got the job at Quartz, before I moved from the Southwest to the East Coast, into an apartment complex that was next to a glinting four-lane highway and had a view of a storage center, before all that I'd been a competitive swimmer. I'd started at the age of twelve, when my mom signed me up at the pool so I'd have something to do while she was at her GRE prep, and I immediately found I had a knack. I remember thinking, This is all you have to do? Just try to keep pushing as hard as you can against the water? Stretch your arm farther than you did the last time and keep doing that? I kept going because I was encouraged and because I became addicted to the approval I saw in the eyes of my coach. I had an instinct, too, that I noticed others didn't have: how to time your first kick after a turn, the arc you sculpt with your hands in the water to get the most pull, minor adjustments that give you just enough of an advantage. I just knew what to do and it felt good.

By the time I was thirteen I was a two-time record setter at the Junior Nationals. I went on to get second and third place for the backstroke at the Nationals in consecutive years. I competed internationally, and when I was only sixteen years old I was ranked sixth in the 100-meter breaststroke at the World Championship Trials in Buffalo. Do you know what that's like? To be sixth best at something in the whole world? I'd lie in bed and think about it. Sixth.

The sixth fastest female swimmer under the age of eighteen. When you took into account the caprice of fate, the random way things jumbled and settled, couldn't sixth, in another variation of the universe with slightly reassembled factors, have been first? Maybe I could have ranked higher—if it wasn't for a kink in my shoulder, and a determination that unexpectedly caved in, one regular morning at college.

It was a Wednesday my junior year at Arizona State, where I was on a full athletic scholarship. I was sitting on the bench, waiting for Coach Serena to write the day's practice sets. I had a queasy-sick feeling from being up so early, something I'd experienced since high school and never been able to overcome. I was in a daze, licking my thumb, staring at the way my thighs pooled on the wooden bench. My shoulder had been clicking. It was a small feeling, something minutely out of place when I brought my arm above my head. I thought it had to do with the angle of my palm in the water and so that week I'd been trying to adjust my stroke. Candace Lancaster was next to me, her head between her legs. I looked at a poster ("LET THEM EAT WAKE") on the wall of the pool room and contemplated whether I should stop by the cafeteria on the way back to my dorm after practice. A few of the other girls walked in from the locker room. There was bulimic Erin Sayers from New Mexico. There was snake-tattoo Kelly from Pennsylvania, and then behind them was someone I'd never seen. She was tall but she looked so young—like a middle-schooler. We made quick eye contact and then she stared aloofly at her nails.

Her name was Stephanie Garcia, and she was a backstroker, like me. I'd worked hard to establish myself on the team, to make myself indispensable. I couldn't believe it when, five minutes later, she surged by in the lane next to me with what seemed like appalling ease. She was like an engine running on cool, mean energy that would never be depleted, a new model that makes you see all the clunky proportions and pulled-out wires of everything else. I tried to catch up, I really tried, but I couldn't.

Five hours a day, six days a week, gouging it out in the hours before school started; the cracked hands, the chlorine hair, the shivering bus rides and random hotel rooms, the fees, the dogged effort of my parents, the year I didn't menstruate, all of it to just be really, really, really good at one thing. And then someone strides in with a kind of poured-gold natural ability; someone who hits the clean, high note you've been struggling for with an almost resentful nonchalance, and the game is over.

You could feel the coaches, even that morning, readjusting their focus, reassembling the team in their minds. I could see how it would all play out—how hard I would have to work, how many more hours I would have to put in, just to maintain my place. Older, shorter, I would never be as good as her. Plus there was my shoulder. I'd been ignoring it, but it was there—a light popping that couldn't be worked out—a button caught somewhere in the works. It would only get worse.

Mentally, I quit that morning. A part of me wondered if I'd been secretly waiting for something like this to happen, or if I wasn't as determined as I always thought I'd been. But it wasn't that. It was an immediate understanding of what was now before me. A lifetime of knowledge and observation served me in one life-changing assessment. I guess I can be grateful that I just knew and didn't delude myself.

It took me a week to say something to Coach Serena. She was the kind of clean, windswept older lady I hoped to be one day. But her manner during our conversation, though perfectly pleasant, confirmed my instincts. She said she was sorry to see me go, and I believed her, but she didn't try very hard to convince me to stay. I stared at a decorative bronze anchor hanging on the wall of her office in a low-lit subbasement of the Memorial Gymnasium as we made the sterile small talk—so different from the years of barky, feral encouragement—that would be our final interaction.

With a year and a half left of college, I found myself beached on a communications degree I had no interest in. When I'd had to pick a major, I'd gleaned from other swimmers that it would be the easiest, but I'd still barely coasted by. I graduated by a hair, and, not knowing what else to do, I moved in with my friend Grace. We had a small one-story house in Tempe. I got a part-time job at a cell phone store—long, silent afternoons behind a counter, or assembling cardboard cutouts of buxom families on their devices. I started coaching, herding little kids in their bathing suits with their big stomachs, talking to parents who lingered after practice. It was all the chaff of the swimming world I'd once dominated, and I realized I had no interest in being on the sidelines. I wanted to shuck it all off.

I went to a career counselor at Alumni Services and she convinced me that the determination I'd exhibited in my swimming career, as well as my communications degree, made me a perfect candidate for some kind of vague position in the business world (she mentioned something like "account manager" and "verticals"), and that moving to the East Coast, where I didn't know anyone save a cousin who bore for me a mutual dislike due to years of forced hanging out at holidays and family reunions, was not a terrible idea.

My second mistake was not doing more research and finding a good place to live. I was moving to a big city, a place I didn't know, but I didn't realize there were neighborhoods where young people were supposed to live. I believed the website of the apartment complex I ended up moving into, called Robins Landing, that said it was a mile from the charming downtown of a sub-city called Arlington. What they didn't tell you was that it was an unwalkable mile of overpasses and parking garages, part of the never-ending Washington, D.C.–area sprawl.

Still, when I first started, I liked the job. I liked the rituals of the working business world, all new to me. I took satisfaction in my painstakingly selected svelte new professional clothes, and striding across the rain-soaked walkway and through the glass doors of the building I worked in. And other little things, like shaking a sugar packet in the break room, and then pouring it into a mug of coffee. I saw myself doing that from the outside, efficiently shaking a sugar packet in my pencil skirt and quarter-inch heels. This is what people did, I thought. They got jobs. They went to meetings. They made friends and exchanged knowing and humorous comments in the hallways about all the same TV shows.

I did hang out with Paula, my cousin, a few times, at her massive house in Silver Spring, Maryland. I'd balance a glass of wine on my lap and sit in the excruciating silence I remembered from our interactions as kids. "Nice bowl," I'd say, pointing to the one on her coffee table. "Is that— Did you make it? Is it made out of clay?" "No," she'd say, wiping something off the corner of her mouth, her red hair scraped back into a bun, her old-man's face as usual just never giving an inch. "It was a gift from Danny."

"Danny . . ."

"Kinsmith. Your other *cousin*? If you ever called him he'd tell you he's taken up ceramics."

I got cable and high-speed Internet. I said hi to my neighbor, a Syrian refugee named Joyce, while getting the mail. I inched forward on the parkway every morning in my car. I bought a lot of frozen dinners and microwaved them and dealt with all the packaging— plastic film and cardboard and compartments that needed to be pushed down in the trash. I sorted through credit card offers and bills and junk mail with the meticulousness of someone with too much free time. The complex had a game room with a pool table and a flat-screen television and sofas, and now and then I'd take a book and go sit and spy on the other tenants, the few who ventured in to watch sports. Or I'd idly sketch the fake holly branches coming out of a vase in an alcove in the wall, and then my hand would pause on the page and I'd look up and see myself from the outside and wonder just how I got slung into this padded room on the damp East Coast, and I couldn't tell if every decision I'd made up to this point, every link that had led me here, had mattered a lot, or hadn't mattered at all.

Back up in my apartment I'd lie in the middle of my living room and toss a small pillow up and down, and think about my virginity, and wonder if it subtly shaped everything I did. Was it possible that people could tell on some frequency, like that pitch or tone that only dogs can hear? Were the un-lubed, un-sexed wheels and gears in me making my movements jerky? And would that quality itself ward men off? I could already feel that happening. Out at a bar, when a guy started talking to me (not that this happened very often), all I could think about was where it was going to go. I wouldn't be able to get into the flow of conversation because I'd imagine the inevitable moment when I'd have to tell him, and how fraught it would then become, and how strange he'd think it was that I'd picked him. Or maybe I wouldn't have to tell him, but was it possible to just play it off? But then my hesitation would read as disinterest and the whole thing would derail from there. I could see what was happening—that the more I obsessed, the more I veered off track. But I couldn't stop. I couldn't relax. And so here I was, twenty-six and bottlenecked in adolescence, having somehow screwed up what came so easily to everyone else, and I couldn't put my finger on *when* this had started happening.

Eleanor Pierce: We're at another sleepover. We're sitting in a circle and talking about sex and who's done it and who hasn't. It's about half and half at that point. Blissfully confident in my youth, I tell the truth, which is that I haven't. "Me neither," said Eleanor. "But I'll kill myself if I'm still a virgin when I'm twenty."

"There's something we've been meaning to tell you," said my father over the phone. I was standing in my kitchen, staring out the window at

suburban Arlington. Silvery, overcast light came in. In the distance, I watched a man in a blue polo shirt push a dolly of boxes along a path through the storage complex next door. He stopped, put his hands on his hips, and looked up at the sky. "Climate Control! U Store U Save First Two Months Free!" it read on the side of one of the units.

After I'd put in my two weeks at Quartz, I'd decided: I was going to move home. I was going to go back to Texas and live with my parents for a little while. I would start over, reassess. At least I knew people there, people who could help me meet other people. I pictured the bright plaza at San Antonio Tech where I used to wait for my mom while she worked on her business degree, the hot benches and spindly trees. Maybe I could take some classes. I thought of the dry, bright air, our sunny kitchen and backyard and the prickly grass, and the smooth, warm stones that lined the walkway up to the shaded porch in the back.

"Your mother and I have decided to rent out our house this summer. We're going to Costa Rica. There are some things we need to work out."

"What?" I said.

"We found a tenant. A nice guy. A carpenter."

"I don't understand," I said.

"What don't you understand?"

"Any of it."

My dad was silent.

"You guys never do stuff like this. And who just rents a random house in a random neighborhood?"

"We found a guy, he's a carpenter."

"You said that."

"People rent things all the time," he said. "You're renting an apartment, are you not?"

This kind of indignant, sideways logic that it was always hard to refute in the moment was my dad's calling card.

"This is different," I said. "You know what I *mean*."

"No I don't. If you're so set on leaving D.C., you could always go stay with your aunt."

"What kind of carpenter? Is he in some sort of recovery program?"

"What? I don't know, Julia, but we've signed an agreement and it's happening."

"What the hell?"

My dad was silent again.

"There's no way I could stay with Helen," I said. "She's a psycho."

"I didn't mean Helen."

"Remember when she painted all those pine cones and flipped out about it?"

"I wasn't talking about Helen."

"Or Miriam. What, does she have like five dog-walking businesses now?"

"I was talking about *my* sister. Vivienne. Remember Vivienne?"

I paused. Three memories came flooding back: Vivienne presenting to me, with quite a lot of fanfare, a framed seashell on some kind of burlap background, and not knowing how I should react; Vivienne getting her hand caught in a glass vase, her fingers squished in its neck like a squid as she developed a fine sheen of perspiration on her forehead; Vivienne's head tilted back thoughtfully against a stone fireplace. Vivienne. Weird, distant Vivienne.

"Oh yeah," I said. "How is she?"

"She's fine. She's still in North Carolina."

"Really?"

My father never talked about his family, or his childhood in the South. His father was an alcoholic, he had a sister who died. A car accident. And that was it. When I pictured his upbringing, which wasn't often, I always imagined a series of sturdy, tired, old people standing next to an overgrown pickup. We'd only ever spent holidays with my mother's side of the family—all the cousins and aunts were hers.

He muffled the phone. "What?" he yelled. He came back. "Your mother wants to talk to you."

"Where in North Carolina?"

"Where I grew up, outside Durham."

"And, I mean, what is she doing?"

"She's fine. She works. She's got a business painting scenes on plates."

"Excuse me?"

"A business. Painting scenes. On plates. She's actually pretty good."

"She paints plates?"

My father sighed. "It would be nice for the two of you to reconnect."

I wasn't sure where this came from. He'd never cared before if I spent time with his relatives.

"Like, dinner plates? Does she make a living that way?"

"Hi, Julia." It was my mom.

"Hi, Mom."

"How are things?"

"Fine," I said. "I heard about your plan."

She cleared her throat. "Yes!"

"Dad said you needed to work out some stuff?"

"Yes, well, no, this isn't . . . We're *fine*."

My parents had been married for a long time. They'd started their own business together, an online retailer called the Trading Post where they sold used saddles, a niche they'd managed to corner, and that drew on my mom's know-how from her riding days when she'd been Collin County's regional gold medal eventing champion. They'd always been dismissive of each other in a way I'd taken for granted and sort of admired. I thought that's the way it was with married adults; you ignored each other all the time in a brassy, warm way. It occurred to me now that maybe it hadn't been so warm.

"I overheard," my mom said. "You're thinking of spending the summer with your aunt?"

"That was just something Dad said."

"Well, it might be nice."

"Yeah, well."

"Have you seen her plates?"

"No," I said. "When would I have done that? Why would I have? I don't even understand what they are."

"She's pretty good at it."

"Yeah, well. No. Nope. I'm not going there. There's no way I'm doing that."

One month later I drove down a thin driveway, gravel popping beneath the tires, toward a house with white columns in the distance. All around stretched raggedy green fields, shiny in the late-day heat. I looked at the piece of paper on which I'd written Vivienne's address: 2705 Three Notched Lane. I had no idea if I was going toward the right place. It had been a while since I'd seen a turnoff, much less a mailbox with an address on it. I passed a large twisted weeping willow. I passed a slumping wire fence. The house, bright in the sun, was on a gentle swell, and behind it was a dark line of trees.

It was only after I'd gotten off the phone with my dad and adjusted to the idea of not being able to go home that the idea of Durham began to take shape. I looked it up and saw that it was a midsize city with a lively downtown area and a historic-district repaving project, and that's when the idea began to take shape. Scrolling through the stock pictures on the tourism part of the website, I saw one of a man and woman laughing at a candlelit dinner. Another showed a couple wearing bright T-shirts and lounging in each other's arms and staring at a hot-air balloon in the sky.

I thought, This is where I'm going to lose my virginity. It would be like going to another country; I would be completely anonymous. I could do whatever I wanted, and it wouldn't be attached to the chain of small failures I'd managed to accrue in Arlington, where I might run into Jessica and Kidman, or in Arizona. I could go to a bar, meet someone off the Internet, join some kind of singles-outing group, whatever. I could be one of these people, walking hand in hand in the sun next to a glass building in a revitalized business district with refurbished cobblestones. I didn't even care that the graceless plan formulating in my head—of just getting it over with, in some anonymous encounter—was so far from how I'd always thought it was going to be, because I was so desperate to get rid of the albatross around my neck. The new plan also had the added incentive of basically being my only option.

I continued slowly along the driveway. A humid breeze came through the windows. It had been a sticky seven-hour drive that included two wrong turns and lunch at a shopping complex where elevator music stood in the air like pond water. Northern Virginia had been a three-lane highway lined with sound walls, which opened up into strip malls, churches, thrift shops, and gun stores as I got farther south. Then it was pretty, sloping fields, and pastures and farms; small towns with deserted streets and mansions set back from the road and fruit stands and dark, closed-down shop fronts. The way got narrower as I approached Durham, and for forty minutes I trailed a truck with two haunted-looking horses inside.

I tried to bring up all my memories of Aunt Viv. I kept thinking of us playing the card game Spit in our kitchen in Texas. I must have been ten or eleven years old. I thought of our hands whirring over the table, over ever-building and eroding piles. Viv is wearing a cotton shirt and she has an air of quiet superiority over her. But I don't mind, because the companionship I felt with her was like being the sidekick to someone immensely capable. I remembered walking slowly through the backyard—she must have been visiting for the summer—and she's pointing out what different plants are called, satisfied by my interest, a soft tower of facts. The feeling I had about her at the time was that she knew a lot of secrets. That there was a funny helix at the center of everything and she was the only one who was aware of it, and she would convey this with an amused side-glance that only you were meant to be in on.

I pulled up, got out of the car, slammed the door, and stretched. I looked around. A hot, wide, creaking day. There was the echo of faraway hammering. In the distance on each side were the trees and fences of other properties. The house was weather-beaten red brick, with a wraparound porch and a copper roof. Weedy wildflowers dotted the grass along the foundation. Three tall windows on the bottom level looked dark. An overgrown path led to what looked like a storage shed.

I went up the porch steps and knocked on the door. Nothing. I crouched down and looked through one of the windows but saw only heavy-looking furniture and dark shapes. I turned around, shaded my eyes from the sun. In the distance, a pickup truck crawled by on the road. I went back down and walked toward my car and was about to get back inside when I heard the door open behind me. I turned around and saw Aunt Viv for the first time in probably sixteen years. I tried to compose my face in the right way.

She walked toward me, smiling. She was wearing a T-shirt tucked into khaki pants. Her face had a scrubbed-fresh, almost abraded quality. Her long, dyed-red hair was swept to the side over one shoulder and tied in a floppy orange bow with fake berries sticking out of the knot. She smiled at me, a warm, conspiratorial smile.

"Julia," she said, in a low, excited way. I remembered that from when I was a kid—how her voice could have a thrilled treble in it. We embraced. We pulled apart and regarded each other. She had aged, and there was a jowly heaviness to her face that hadn't been there before, but you could still see the shadings of the girl she had been, how I'd remembered her from long ago—when she'd been pretty in a sort of game, clear-eyed way. "That's a pretty bow," I said, and then for some reason: "Did you make it?"

Her hand shot up, touched it. Something, ever so slightly, dismantled itself in her expression.

"Oh," she said, "does it look that way?"

"No, in a good way!"

She smiled again, recomposed. "Look at you," she said. "Come on up. I'll show you your room."

I leaned my suitcase against the wall and looked around. I was in a sparse, clean room with faded wallpaper. After we'd made some small talk about the trip, Viv had led me up the creaking stairs. "Well," she said, "I'll let you get settled. The bathroom is just down the hall." She hesitated, then left.

I walked over to the bed and hauled my suitcase on top of it. There were two windows, surrounded by frilly curtains. I opened one. The room bloomed with warm, humid air. The wallpaper was a pattern of beige and pink flowers. The furniture was all wooden and looked antique, handed down. There was a white-painted chest of drawers that let out a musty smell when I opened them, a closet, a small wicker desk, and a night table with a decorative pitcher on it. It all had the feeling of a slightly moldering bed-and-breakfast, down to the little satchels of potpourri leaning against a mirror. I stared at a framed poster that read "The 1976 Newport Jazz Festival," which showed a flower piping out some musical notes. I picked up a heavy silver jewelry dish with rippling sides.

I unpacked and went to the bathroom. I sat on the squeaking bed and stared straight ahead. Then I lay on my stomach and looked out at the field and the trees in the distance, and the hazy yellow late-day sky, and tried not to feel like a rope had been cut, and I could only tell it had ever been there by the new sense of drifting.

Half an hour later, I wandered down the stairs and found Viv in the kitchen, savagely mixing something in a small bowl with a towel slung over her shoulder.

"Can I help with anything?" I said.

"No," she said distractedly, and then gestured toward the table. "There's wine if you like. The opener should be in one of those drawers."

I busied myself looking for it, rummaging around. I couldn't tell—should we be talking, making small talk, laughing and catching up at this point? Everything I did seemed too loud. "Here it is," I said to fill the silence, when I found the opener.

I hovered for a moment, and then wandered into the adjacent living room—a dim area with a cinnamon air-freshener smell and pashmina shawls draped over things. I sat down for a moment, then got up. I looked at a frame with a bunch of seashells hot-glued to it. I thought of our hands whirring over the cards. We'd had a few pleasant, polite phone conversations in the weeks leading up to my arrival, and I wouldn't have thought it would be like this, like it was fifteen minutes later when we sat quietly across from each other at a long table in the red dining room under a badly tilting brass chandelier. She chewed quickly. Her hair was parted down

the middle and tied back. She had changed clothes—she was wearing a shirt with pastel handprints on it. Her nails were painted red
and she looked abrasively clean.

"Wow, this all looks great," I said.

"Good," said Aunt Viv. She arranged a napkin in her lap. She
smiled. I smiled. I took a sip of my water.

"I really like my room," I said.

"Good, good," she said. She nodded expectantly, like I was supposed to say more. Like something more was supposed to happen
in that moment.

"I was looking at that poster," I said. "Do you like jazz?"

"You do?" she said politely.

"No, I mean, do you? I was asking if you do."

"If I . . ."

"Like jazz. Jazz music. Are you a fan?"

It dawned on her. She tried to shimmy herself into the conversation. "Oh, oh of course," she said, waving her fork, squinting. "I've
tried, you know?"

"Sure, yeah," I said.

She nodded and went back to her food.

"Dad says you paint plates?" I said.

"Yes," she said, dabbing the side of her mouth with a napkin.
"'My little hobby,' right?"

"Oh, no, no," I said. "He didn't say it like that."

She shrugged, and sawed at her chicken.

"But so, you do?" I said. "You do do that?"

"I do, yes," she said. "I do." I had a flash of her cracking up with my dad on the sidewalk outside our house as they tried to hold on to whipping and wheeling sheets of poster board in the wind. There are gray clouds in the background. She's laughing helplessly, her eyes shining, their efforts futile against the forces.

"Do you sell them?"

"More and more," she said. "I do series, themes, you know. Different things each time. I'm trying to get it off the ground. But for now, for my day job, I still do hospice work."

"Oh, okay," I said. "What's that like?"

She shrugged. "Tiring." She looked around. She had ramrod posture and a large forehead and a feminine, voluptuous face, but there was a shiny hardness there, too, as if there were steel rods beneath her skin.

I turned my napkin over in my lap, took a sip of wine, flicked something off the table. I glanced up at the brass chandelier and wondered about the likelihood of it crashing to the table. The seconds ticked by.

She seemed to remember I was there. She smiled brightly. "What do you think you'll be doing here," she said, "for the summer?"

"Well, I have to get a job. But I'm also planning on writing an essay," I said, surprising myself, the idea having only occurred to me right then.

"Really?"

"Yes," I said, "about swimming. About swimming culture. What it's like. I don't think there's much out there—or at least I haven't read much—about what it's like. And I have that firsthand experience."

"Of course," she said. She stared thoughtfully into the distance. "I remember that period of time. Hilary always talked about that. How driven you were. She was really impressed."

I shrugged and nodded.

"She'd talk about how you'd wake her up, drag her out of bed. You were all ready to go. You just wanted to get there. How you begged them to let you sign up at the swim team."

"She said that?"

Viv nodded.

"That I begged them to sign up?"

"Yes."

"But"—I shook my head—"that's . . . They were the ones who wanted me to do it."

She shrugged, chewed.

"I thought, because of Mom's failed horse-riding career. I mean, *she* was the one who signed me up, you know, initially."

I thought of my mom watching me from the bleachers at practice, biting her thumbnail, her face knitted with inner calculations. I thought of the subtle way she'd let me know if she thought I'd done a good job or not: if I could watch television in the living room when we got home, the meted-out dessert portions after dinner, the grade of affection in her voice when she said good night. Had I imagined all that? Everything tilted ominously as I considered that a huge portion of my life may have been based on a misunderstanding.

"Anyway," I said, trying to figure out how to change the subject.

"Wasn't there talk of you going to the Olympics?" she said.

"I went to the Olympic trials in Tallahassee," I said.

She nodded, and I was annoyed by the way she gingerly avoided probing any further, as if it was something I was sensitive about, some huge failure that I hadn't made it to the actual Olympics. People didn't know. They didn't know how good you had to be to even get to the trials. I wrenched apart a roll.

"Do you do a lot of crafts?" I said. "I noticed a few knickknacks around the house. Like that frame, in the living room?" I couldn't tell if she'd heard me. She was methodically pulling something apart on her plate. "With the seashells on it? Or is that from— Do you travel a lot?" I said desperately.

Viv cleared her throat and looked up. "I took a class," she said.

"Oh, okay."

"On frame decoration."

"I see." I waved my fork around. "So, they said you could do pretty much whatever you wanted? With the frames?"

She glanced up at me. She straightened her shoulders. "Yes," she said primly. She repositioned a piece of chicken with her knife and fork. I mashed a pea on my plate.

I looked up at the chandelier and said a little prayer that it actually would come crashing down.

"I did used to travel, quite a bit," she said. "In fact, I recently went to Orlando."

"Florida? What was that like?"

"Very lively." She finished chewing and again dabbed the sides of her mouth. "I stayed with a friend there. A very nice apartment complex. It had balconies with"—she shaped the air with her hands—"flower boxes. And"—she continued shaping the air—"all different colors, as if to get the effect of a village. One evening a young man, he turned out to be divorced, invited us into the court-yard and we had teriyaki, all together there."

She looked at me expectantly.

I nodded frantically. "Great," I said. "Cool—so, he was a chef?"

"Yes," she said. I felt as if I had disappointed her in some funda-mental way. "More or less."

"Great."

The rest of dinner, we couldn't find a toehold. I gave her an up-date about how Mom and Dad were doing. I talked blandly about my old job at Quartz. She perfunctorily told me about her duties at the hospice where she worked, talking to families and dealing with patients. I worked hard to keep her going about this, pumping her with questions, because it seemed like safe territory—work. And it distracted us from what I think she must have been feeling, too. That we'd lost whatever ease we'd had when I was a kid and she came to visit us in Texas.

Back up in my room, I poked around online for a while and then tried to read. At ten o'clock I turned off the lamp and lay there with my eyes open. A breeze came in and ruffled some of the pages of a spiral notebook on the bureau. It must have been two hours before I was finally able to drift off, listening to the shifting, digestive sounds of the house at night, and trying not to feel like I'd made a terrible mistake.

—Two—

When was the last time you wanted something? Wanted it so badly that the very grip of your wanting seemed to prevent you from actually getting it because you were throwing things off with your need, holding too hard, jarring things out of joint?

The next day I sat in the sun on the front porch, wondering how I was going to do it—how I was going to lose my virginity.

Aunt Viv had left for work before I woke up and I'd explored her home and the yard. I'd found some rubber boots in a hall closet and skirted the perimeter of the land in the back, weeds and tall grass whipping against my shins. A small trail led into the woods, and I went along on it until I came to an overgrown trailer that looked like a dining car from the 1950s. I peered in the windows, which were almost fully opaque with dirt and dust, and inside saw the outline of piles of wood. I kept going on the trail until it went under a fence and I had to turn around.

Back out in the sun, I kept going until I came to a twisted-up oak tree. I sat on the roots for a little while, watching everything in its hot summer stillness, grateful to be in the shade.

I went into the barn, where there were plastic chairs, and a few tables, and a bed frame, and some old wreaths, and sharp slats of light on the floor. There were cans of paint and jars and canvases. Something big and bulky was covered in a dusty tarp. I felt a small sting on the back of my leg. I slapped it and left.

Down the long gravel driveway, at the mailbox, I looked back and forth along the street. In the distance, ivy crawled along the power lines. The day bore down. I walked back to the house, feeling heavy and disorganized with heat. I got some water and then came back out and sat on the porch.

My virginity composed about 99 percent of my thought traffic. I concentrated on it—trying to drill it down to its powder, its particle elements, trying to recategorize it, impose different narratives on why this had happened.

I *knew* the way it worked, too—that certain attitudes would attract certain things. I knew that if you ignored something, stepped away from it, allowed yourself to breathe, it would come to you. It was like when I worked the box office at San Antonio Stage one summer, and I had to open the wonky combination lock to the safe, and sometimes the harder I tried, the more stuck it would get. But if I gave it a moment, allowed myself to float away, I had that necessary confidence, finesse, whatever that thing is that certain dim athletes and movie stars have—that insouciance that causes all the cogs in your universe to sync, gives you easy passage. The lock would click.

And that was the problem—to want something so badly was to jam yourself into the wrong places, gum up the works, send clanging vibrations into the cosmos. But how can you step back and affect nonchalance?

When I really wanted to torture myself I'd think of Eddie Avilas. He was the guy who, in high school, had most closely resembled someone you could call my boyfriend. And what really stung me about it, thinking back, was his general optimism and knee-jerk decency, how I hadn't realized what a nice person he was.

I would remember the time he squeezed each of my fingertips on the dusty blue tarp in the middle of the track field. His tiny kitchen and terrifying father. His strange jeans. The beat-up neon-yellow lunch satchel he would always bring to school. (It was only in hindsight that I realized Eddie was extremely poor.) How he would feel like a pile of firewood, all jangly and warm, lying on top of me when we were watching a movie in my basement.

There was the time we were in his small sunlit kitchen with our homework spread out in front of us on the table. We reached a kind of lull, or resting point, in the conversation and he does this *thing*. I sort of see it from the corner of my eye and then look over, and through some glint of intuition I know that he wants me to see as he tosses his pen up into a flip and then expertly catches it. He looks at me with eyes as hopeful and pliable as a baby bird's, but there's also a gleam of pride there. This all happened very quickly, but so much occurred to me in that moment—that he had been practicing this move and waiting for a chance to perform it when it would seem most offhand and casual, like he just had this facility with the world, this capability that he wanted me to see. And in that moment he needed my approval so much that it was embarrassing, and instead of doing what I should have done, which was to just *give him that* by some flicker of awe or grin of admiration, I ignored him. And he saw me deciding to ignore him. And I guess you could say that it wasn't a big deal, but a part of me knew that it was in these small transactions that unkindness could be most felling. I would have given anything to go back.

But that wasn't even the worst part. The worst part happened a few months later in a hotel pool in Corpus Christi. Because a few of our friends were going, Eddie and I got roped into a beach trip spearheaded by this Christian organization that was always sponsoring events at our high school. Despite the religious underpinnings, we had heard that the beach trip was basically a free-for-all. It was one of the few weekends I didn't have a swim meet, so we signed up.

When we got there, however, it wasn't long before we figured out that it was going to be a super-structured weekend of indoctrination. The second night we were all corralled into a conference room or ballroom-type area at the hotel where we were all staying, and made to watch a Christian punk band play against a bunch of depressingly stacked chairs. Eddie and I managed to sneak out.

We ran through the carpeted hallways. We made out against the empty breakfast buffet in the deserted dining room. We found a sitting area centered around a display of mystery novels and a small tree in a geometric pot. Hopped up on the warm hotel air and sense of escape, we decided to find the roof. Instead we found the pool.

It was deserted, bright, humid, and sultry with a shrine-like stillness and a fake, spiky tree in each corner. We tested the water and it was warm. We stripped down to our underwear and climbed in. Eddie got out, sculpted his wet hair into a Mohawk, and cannonballed. We breathed into each other's mouths underwater.

At a certain point, we were kissing against the side, sitting on an underwater outcropping, like a stair or a ledge. Eddie pulled back and said to me, "Do you want to?" He said it without any pressure, as if this was just a one-time thing, a toss-off, the perfect crest to our little escape, and not something we'd slowly, languidly been building toward. He said it with warmth, a sense of adventure.

I spent a lot of time thinking back and trying to trace the exact pathways of logic or reasoning that led me to, after considering it for a few humid seconds, coyly decline. It's not like I didn't *want* to—we had been slowly kissing for a while. It could have been that something about the cold lapping of the water, a less comfortable temperature than it had been before, along with a smudged pelican fixture that seemed to be staring at us from the wall combined to tip the atmosphere just enough the wrong way. It could have been that the stampeding intimacy of not only that moment but the whole half hour before was just too much, and I felt that I just needed a second. But what I think it really was—because I was on the knife's edge, it really could have gone either way—was that I figured this was just the tip of the iceberg. That this was surely the beginning of many similar escapades. That I could *afford* to decline, if only to make the next proposition all the more delicious.

How could I have known how wrong I was?

So I told him, "Not tonight," and pushed back, swimming away. It didn't seem like a big deal at the time; Eddie smiled at me quizzically and we hung out for a little longer and then got out, but things never culminated for us in the same way again. I kept assuming they would, but I think he thought he had been too pushy, and I was too shy to bring it up. It was as if that moment kicked off a series of misunderstandings that caused us to fall slightly out of step. He went away for the summer and by the time he got back things had ramped up for me swimming-wise; I hardly had any free time, and that was that.

I began to think of that moment, when I pushed away from him and swam to the other side of the pool, as being where my fate changed, where I branched off and started living a parallel life that wasn't supposed to be.

In the other life, having lost my virginity at a young age in a hotel pool, I'm sexed and supple and swanning through a series of relationships, through life. The hang-up of losing my virginity would never have impeded me. It would never have started to worry me, only slightly at first, but then more and more as my friends each lost theirs and I got older and it seemed that I had lost some beat, some essential rhythm.

It would never have been something that started to curdle inside me, that I started to think about all the time. I'm a twenty-four-year-old virgin, I'd think, as I hit my hip on a gate and sneezed at the same time. I'm a twenty-five-year-old virgin, staring at the tiles of a mural on a city street. I'm a twenty-six-year-old virgin, catching my reflection in a car window.

Untouched. Like a flower suffocating in its own air. Like something pickling in its own juices. Something that badly needed to be turned inside out, banged right.

I watched a bumblebee leadenly explore a rose next to the porch. In the distance were the faint sounds of construction, something grinding and then hammering.

I thought, The further down this path I go, the more freakish I'll become. The stranger of a species I'll be, curling with my own horrible, weird hair. It was time to jam the key into the lock and force it, because I didn't have time to step back and meditate my way onto the right path.

I needed to make a plan for the summer, a surefire strategy. I had to shed whatever preconception I had before about how it was all going to *be*.

— *Three* —

I stood in a room in Viv's house filled with hanging plates. There was a tall cabinet in the corner, and on top of that was a clock embedded in what looked like a porcelain flower bank. It ticked heavily.

The plates were lined up in sets of four or five, and on each one was a meticulously painted scene. There was a jellyfish, painted in purples and pinks, gliding through the water toward the surface. It was part of a series that had to do with the ocean. Another one showed a craggy turquoise mountain under the sea. Another an underwater city, with clusters of towers and twinkling lights. A school of fish swam through, giving a sense of scale.

A different group showed a bright, teeming garden outside some kind of ominous estate with dark windows. There were twisting rosebushes, sculpted shrubs, and orange paths; flowers spewed out of small pots and the tops of statues. The perspective was all off, as if a child had done it. It was like the ground leading up to the estate was tipped up, slanted wrong. One plate showed the property from a different side, where a gray wall cast a shadow across a birdbath, and it looked like someone had just left a picnic, a golden fork and knife strewn on the ground. They were meticulously detailed. You could see the designs, some flicks of a thin brush, on the pots, and the small wells of shadows on the statues.

Other plates showed scenes of horses and cowboys, migrating bison and teepees on great plains, a Wild West theme. In another series was a line of camels following a colorful sultan across the desert, their bodies making long shadows across the sand.

It wasn't so hard to see why people would buy these. On each of them were Viv's tiny initials, "V.G." My favorites, or the ones I stared at the longest, depicted two mice constructing a multi-tiered card house on a red carpet in a dark living room. In the last plate, a mouse was standing on its tiptoes, balancing the final one on top. You could see tiny dots on each card—spades, hearts; it must have taken forever. Next to each mouse was a gold goblet. I stared at them for a really long time.

I then wandered with my laptop into the sunroom, a frayed, faded area with a row of windows you could crank open. There was a pouchy purple velvet couch and a glass coffee table with some craft books stacked on it.

Here was the list I made:

 – Take some kind of community class
 – Hang around the university or audit a course
 – Internet dating
 – Go to a bar
 – Join a gym
 – Go to a sales conference or a convention at a local hotel
 – Join a singles-outing group
 – Take a language class

- Get a job
- Don't think too much
- Just be relaxed about it

I studied the profile picture of a man with the screen name "The-MeeksShallInherit." He was outside, at what appeared to be an electronics fair, standing next to a table with a neon-orange tablecloth on it. There was another picture of him against the Golden Gate Bridge. Then a picture of him holding a huge kite and giving the thumbs-up.

"He sounds like an alien. Those are the kinds of pictures an alien would put up," said Grace, my old roommate whom I'd lived with in Tempe and who was now my closest friend.

"Really?" I said.

"To convince you he was human and knows how to do things."

"Sure," I said.

I clicked through a few more pictures.

"Well, at least he's not holding a huge pencil at an imaginarium," I said. "Like, 'Look at me!'"

"Totally."

After I'd left, she'd stayed in Arizona and gotten a job at the historic public library in Tucson. I'd been there once. As we talked, I could hear her heels click on the marble floor as she walked around in the giant, day-lit atrium.

"He's sent me a bunch of messages. Lots of exclamation points. He seems really jazzed about everything."

"Well," she said, "that's not a bad quality, necessarily."

I could feel her choosing her words. I'd let her think, over the years, by alluding to it or not correcting her when she made assumptions, that I'd had sex. That I'd been having sex. But there was something about the wide berth she gave the subject that made me think she knew the truth. Once, when she'd visited me, I told her about a flirtation I had at Quartz to keep apace with a story she was telling, and a troubled, questioning look had come over her face.

"So what's she like?" she said. "Your aunt?"

"She's nice," I said. "She's polite. She's got a kind of inner poise. She's very poised."

"Okay."

"She's artistic. She has been to Orlando."

"Okay."

"Recently."

"Got it."

I heard the shrieks of children over the phone. A school group, bustling by.

"You're really painting a nuanced picture," she said.

"There's a sort of hard quality to her. Like, if you said, 'What do I do with this hen that's bullying all the other chickens?' and you were having all these qualms, she would take it from you and snap its neck, just like that."

"So she has leadership qualities?"

"I'm not *not* saying that."

"I get it."

"I do think she'd be a good person to have in some survival situation. Like some kind of space mission that crash-landed on another planet and lost touch with Earth."

"I'd be like, 'Might as well rampage through the dessert rations!'" said Grace.

"Me too," I said. "Except if it was only little boxes of golden raisins. In which case I'd be like, 'Has anyone gone ahead and tried these cyanide tablets?' Oh, hey, Aunt Viv."

She stood in the doorway. I hadn't heard her come in.

"Grace," I said, "I have to go." I put down the phone.

She was wearing a sheer white cotton overshirt-type thing that seemed to float around her body.

"Hi." She looked around the room. "I didn't know you'd be in here."

"Yeah, I— It's nice and calm."

"I agree." She tried on a bright smile. "Did you have a nice day? I was afraid you'd be bored."

"No, I got a lot of writing done," I lied. "It was great. No, this is just what I was hoping it would be like."

"Good, good."

We both looked at my bare feet, which were up on the coffee table. I lowered them. She pinched her ear. "It's my friend Alice's birthday tomorrow. She's having a small get-together. I was wondering if you'd like to come?"

There was a slight quaver beneath her veneer that made me realize that perhaps she, too, had thought our conversation at dinner the other night had been lacking and that she was trying to make up for it, reaching out.

"Sure, yeah," I said. "What time?"

"Three o'clock. In the afternoon."

I nodded with a little too much exaggeration. "Great."

"Great," she said.

And then, because the moment seemed to require something more, I said, "I really like your plates. The hanging-up ones? In that room? They're really good."

"Thank you," she said. "Those are from earlier. When I was first starting."

"Oh, okay."

She hesitated in the doorway. Then we started talking at the same time. "So, did you just get home?" I said. She said, "I've actually submitted a few of my latest ones to an art show."

"What?" I said.

"I've submitted a few. To an art show. I'm doing a series about Arthurian legend. The Knights of the Round Table."

"Cool," I said. "Great. Like a local, community type of deal?"

"Well," she said. I had insulted her. Something shifted between us and I immediately felt terrible. I also realized why Viv's first impulse was to pull back and be aloof, because otherwise her face would unlock and every raw emotion would visibly travel across it. In this case, she flashed with hurt.

"It's actually much bigger than that," she said. "It's sponsored by the folk art museum of Durham. It's widely known. Have you heard of *Southern Living* magazine?"

"I think so," I said quickly.

"Well, they do a feature."

"That's awesome," I said. "That's really cool. So are you—"

"Well, I'm going to eat something," she said. "There are leftovers in the fridge." And then she turned around and walked away.

And that was how I ended up driving into town the next day with Aunt Viv in her Honda Civic. It was hot and bright and everything was bursting with full summer lushness, the sky a chesty blue.

"Alice is in the last stages of lymphoma," she said.

"Oh." I was picking the sticky protective shield off the screen of my cell phone. I put it down and looked at her. "That's horrible. I'm sorry."

"Well, she's got a good support system."

"How long have you known her?"

"Many years," said Viv. "We worked together."

She was wearing diamond-shaped emerald earrings and her hair was swept back into an elegant French braid.

She glanced at me. "Have you spoken to your parents?"

"A little," I said. "They seem to be doing fine. They're, like, meditating every day and doing psychic weaving with a shaman or something."

This little dash of sarcasm did not seem to go over with Aunt Viv. It was quiet for a while. We passed someone hanging up a row of small white dresses for a yard sale.

"It must be very interesting," she said. "It must be a very interesting culture. There in South America."

"Yes. Yes! It must be," I said, nodding. "So, would you— Is that somewhere you'd want to go?"

"Perhaps," she said. "I think I'd rather go to Europe. Verona. I haven't really been out of the country much."

"Why there?"

"The music," she said. "The opera at the outdoor amphitheater, with everyone holding candles at night." She sang a tune, a few notes of something, as if she were in a daydream, and then looked at me expectantly. My eyes darted around the car.

We drove along a street with many old Southern mansions set way back from the road. After a while we turned onto a narrower street, with smaller houses, and pulled up in front of a shady, flower-petal-covered walkway.

We got out of the car at the same time as a woman with long, earth-mother gray hair who was carrying some kind of pickled thing leaking out of a plastic bag and so had to hurry in ahead of us.

We were greeted at the door by a large woman named Karen wearing a purple dress with many layers. Her face was filled with happiness, her eyes dancing, her cheeks flushed. "Vivi!" she said, and then gave my hand a vigorous shake.

She led us down a hallway into a living room with zebra pillows and decorative spears on the walls and other foreign-looking arti-facts. Viv introduced me around, and then the crowd parted to re-veal Alice, swaddled in purple scarves, sitting stoically in a wicker chair like a village elder or seer.

She had a weak chin and warm brown eyes, and a trembling shine about her—like a bulb of water on a leaf right before it breaks. She smiled up at me and said, "I'm so glad to meet one of Viv's rel-atives." Viv knelt down beside her and took one of her hands and held it like it was the most fragile thing in the world while her face broke into a smile of bald admiration and sadness.

I said hello and then backed away to give Aunt Viv and Alice some room, and then weaved back through the house to find something to drink. It felt like I was intruding to stay talking to them longer. I was wearing tights even though it was a hot day, and they were itchy and sagging down and I had an eyelash in my eye.

"This was my aunt Cassie," said a woman named Diane, who had intercepted me and then led me into a room—it was her house—where she showed me how she'd lacquered old pictures of her relatives onto the top of her desk. Cassie stared sternly out from a rocking chair.

"Great," I said.

"And this is my great-grandfather Francis. They called him Franny."

"Oh, okay."

Diane obviously had a lot of time on her hands. I sensed she had more money than the other women. From what I'd gathered, they were all part of a core friend group that met while working at a hospice before it closed.

"It's so I can have them all around me," she said, sweeping her hand around the room. "All my ancestors, whispering from the eaves."

"Yeah," I said, smiling, trying to seem appropriately receptive to that concept. "I can see how that would be nice."

After about twenty minutes, I managed to extract myself by saying I was thirsty and wanted to get some water. Then I slalomed between a few other people who looked like they wanted to talk and ended up positioning myself by a set of glass shelves. I pulled out various photography books and pretended to look at them, but really I was studying the women.

I watched Karen—the one who greeted us—walk around offering people cups of juice, stopping now and then to chat. Her arms were mottled red and she had a bustling and helpful way about her. I wondered if that's how she'd be in bed—cheerfully helping things along in a brusque and no-nonsense manner, like a fishwife who'd seen it all. She would probably just want to get to the next thing and it wasn't that complicated. I wondered if she was married and thought about how the right man could have a lot of happiness with a woman like that. She wasn't what you would call attractive in a conventional sense, but now and then she shrieked with laughter and seemed to find mischievous humor in everything and you could probably have a kind of ribald joy with her of the kind that wasn't seen in movies or porn.

I watched Diane massage the back of her neck and tilt her head serenely to the side while talking to someone. She was sort of beautiful in a strategically tousled way. She had a self-consciously throaty manner, like she wanted the world to know how deeply she felt things. I imagined she was really theatrical in bed and had deep, oaky orgasms and saw herself from the outside the whole time and threw a bunch of colored scarves into the air when she came.

Then there were people you couldn't imagine having sex. I studied a woman sitting on the couch whom I hadn't been introduced to. She had the prim face of a prairie schoolteacher and was irritably rummaging through a lime-green bag. She pulled out a bunch of receipts and pawed through them in her hand. I noticed middle-aged women like that sometimes. They'll be wearing a hand-crafted vest over a turtleneck or something and pretty much expressing to the world that sex or the idea of sex was generally not on the table. But I couldn't tell if, this lady for instance, if she had done this to herself or if everyone else had done it to her.

My thoughts were interrupted by Karen. We got into a conversation about how her father had been a door-to-door salesman in Nevada.

"'It's a forgotten art,' is what he always used to say," she said.

"Gosh," I said, thinking about walking around hot, flat, grid-shaped neighborhoods wearing a business suit.

"How long do you think you'll be staying with your aunt?" she said, turning back to me and reaching for an olive. We were now standing in the kitchen, where some snacks had been laid out.

"A few months, until the end of summer."

A wistful look came over her face. She looked into the distance. "You're lucky."

"What do you mean?"

"To get to spend so much time with Vivienne. She's such an adventurous soul."

"Yeah," I said, somewhat confused.

"We were all so impressed when we heard about Bora Bora."

"Bora Bora?"

She nodded, popped a cube of cheese into her mouth. "You know, not that many people would do what she did—just go and live there by themselves for a year. It takes a lot of guts. She's hilarious about it, too. The coconut pantomime? You should ask her about it. I wish I could have gone."

"Yeah," I said, impressed. "I will."

Someone came up to us and said it was probably a good time to start thinking about serving the cupcakes and our conversation ended.

I talked to a few more people, and then wandered around a little with a cup of juice. I was studying some framed pressed flowers when I happened to look over and see Aunt Viv talking to a group of the women. She was holding up a decorative crystal goblet—the light glinted through it—and telling a story. She was talking quickly. Her hair was coming out of her braid a little, and her face was flushed. It was something funny; the people listening were giggling and paying close attention. I could see that in this context, with these women, she had a kind of power. She was presiding, divvying out attention and eye contact while they all stood around with open faces. Everyone burst out laughing at the same time, and she looked around in a happy, calculating way.

Later, in the car, I asked her about it.

"So you went to Bora Bora?"

"What?" she said, looking over at me, bemused.

"Didn't you live there for a year?"

"Me?"

"Yeah. Karen said—about the coconut pantomime?"

"Oh." She reddened. She became visibly flustered. She started messing with the radio dial and accidentally hit the turn signal, which started clicking.

"This *thing*," she said, annoyed, poking at it, and then the wind-shield wipers came on.

"So you went there?" I said, prompting her again, once she'd turned them off and a few moments had passed.

She nodded quickly without looking at me. The atmosphere in the car became warped and strange. We sat in silence the rest of the way.

It was only later that night, thinking back on the incident and trying to decipher her behavior that I realized what had happened. Aunt Viv had acted exactly like someone caught in a lie. She'd never gone to Bora Bora. She'd made up a story and then forgotten about it until I brought it up. I thought of the imperious way she presided over her friends at the party, how she basked in their admiration; her obvious pleasure as she conducted the moment, and the look of triumph on her face when they burst out laughing. I could see embellishing a little bit, but what kind of person would make up a story that outlandish completely out of nowhere? What did Viv want the world to think of her?

— *Four* —

I stared at a colossal man named Ed Branch. He was like a mountain in a swivel chair. His huge face appeared to be melting, his cheeks sagging, the shiny skin under his eyes dripping down in two wide, flat drops. He was smiling at me in a jovial way. I took a sip from a glass of water on the heavy mahogany desk in front of me. There was a framed picture of an equally robust person—his wife, I assumed—caught unawares and laughing with a watering can, her face plump and happy, and I imagined they regularly had bawdy, baseboard-pounding sex, and then every once in a while she would watch him doing little boyish things, and her heart would burst.

And then there was Wes, sitting next to him. Wes seemed like a nice guy, too. He was young, grave, and ex-military. He had a knee-jerk politeness about him, old-fashioned and Southern. I wondered if that meant he'd be the same in bed, attentive to your every need with perfect decorum. Or maybe that consideration could turn cold and sharpen into cruelty. I wondered if this was something you could tell about a person.

"What was it you said you did at this Quartz Consulting?" said Ed. His hand absently wandered over to a nut bowl.

I was interviewing with them for a job at a firm called Kramer Branch, a week after I'd arrived in Durham. My third day there, with Viv gone again, the house quiet, I was stretched like a piano string. Everything had sputtered out—the essay I started writing; it was too hot to go for a walk. I tried reading in different rooms, but I couldn't get into a book. I ended up in the sunroom, feeling half deranged, looking at a dusty craft manual on weaving. Finally, in defeat, I pulled over my laptop and started looking for part-time work. Plus, I thought, how was I ever even going to *meet* people? I needed to get out of this house and into town.

This job, part-time afternoon receptionist, was the first thing that had come up for which I looked remotely qualified, and I'd only have to come in after one o'clock every day.

"I facilitated communications by sourcing available online assets about solutions on higher education and applied them to a dynamic Web portal," I said. "I was the social media pulse of the entire company."

Wes and Ed looked at each other uncomfortably.

"Well," said Ed, "what we really need here is someone to answer the phones for the afternoon shift. Run the odd errand."

"I think I would thrive at that," I said.

Two days later I was in my business clothes, making the twenty-minute drive back there for my first afternoon. The offices were in an old dry-goods store next to the train tracks, repurposed and outfitted with beige carpeting and wallboard and new windows in shiny plastic sashes. I walked inside, letting the glass door sigh shut behind me. Midday light came through some blinds and striped the floor. It was quiet except for an ambient electric drone. I looked around—maybe everyone had gone to lunch. I walked past a fraying taupe sofa and a glass coffee table with dingy magazines and up to the front desk, behind which was sitting one of the oldest people I'd ever seen in my life. She had sparse, short gray hair. She was wearing a patterned prairie dress with a frilly collar. Her face was an elaborate network of wrinkles and she looked wind-beaten, like she'd spent her life wandering through desert cliffs. She was trying to pull some cotton out of a huge bottle of vitamins, and her glasses were about to fall off her nose, and everything about her seemed to be teetering on the verge of disaster and I wasn't sure if I should help or intervene in any way.

I stood there and waited for her to notice me. She teased out some strands of cotton.

"Excuse me?" I said. No response.

"Hello?" I said, and then, after a moment, "Can I help with that?"

Still nothing.

I stared at a plushy stuffed dog sitting up and hanging its legs over the edge of the table.

I was about to go knock on a door when I heard someone bustling down the stairs. It was a woman with a helmet of gray hair wearing flowing pastel vacation clothes. "Hi there," she said. She arrived in front of me and extended her arm and about fifty bangles slid down. "You must be Julia."

"Hi, yes," I said, shaking her hand.

She turned to the old lady.

"Caroline," she said.

Nothing.

"Caroline!" She banged on a desk bell a bunch of times.

The old lady looked up. "Jeannette," she said loudly.

Jeannette took the vitamins from her and yanked out the cotton and gave them back. "This is Julia," she said loudly. "She's our new afternoon receptionist."

"Hi," I said.

We stared at each other.

Jeannette and I went up the stairs. "She's James Kramer's mother," she said. She glanced at me sideways and rolled her eyes. "She used to be a judge. Down in Florida? Now she helps out around here." And then, as an afterthought, as if she felt bad: "A lot of grit there. A lot of wisdom."

"Sure," I said.

We walked around and she pointed out all the things I would have to do each day. I was to keep track of the supply closet, water the plants, make sure the conference rooms were ready when there was going to be a meeting by putting coffee out, answer the phones at the front desk for a few hours, dust a row of glass clocks that were awarded at a yearly conference, run a package up to the titles office on Green Street now and then, and other low-grade tasks. Since there wasn't much to say about the job, most of our conversation centered around the cruise Jeannette had just taken with her husband.

"Did anyone jump overboard?" I said.

She shrieked with laughter. "No, hon," she said.

"Was all the food free?"

"It was, it was. And get this, there was a different ice sculpture in the shrimp every night. I said to Ken, I said, 'What do they do with the old ones? Lick 'em?'"

I laughed. "That's right," I said. "They just lick them down."

"They say, 'Now lemme get that shrimpy ice thing. I wanna lick it!'"

We both cracked up, with her elbowing me in the ribs a little. I thought I had found a kindred spirit, and later I would be a little crestfallen to realize that Jeannette had this dynamic with pretty much everyone and would laugh at anything you said as long as it was under your breath and in a secretive manner.

I met Wes again. He was on the phone and gave me a polite nod. Ed Branch was tenderly pruning an office plant. I was introduced to a paralegal roughly my age named Allison Block. She looked up from her salad in a friendly way and shook my hand over her desk. I met James Kramer for the first time. He was on the phone and waved us away.

Just like that the flurry of activity was over and I was sitting at the front desk, by myself, in the quiet. I could see a pebble walkway through the glass front door. I was on the ground floor of the building, and something about the awning outside, and the way the light slanted in, gave the impression of the room filling up with shade from the ground up, like an aquarium would with water. Everything was becoming submerged: the taupe sofa, the coffee table, a picture in a heavy brass frame. I swiveled around in my chair. I checked my e-mail. I contemplated quitting, if not tomorrow then the day after that. Because what was I doing in this staid, afternoon-y place when what I should really be doing was working at a restaurant or something like that—a place with people my

age and alcohol and energy and lines that could be crossed? I probably would have made up some excuse and found a way out, if it
wasn't for what happened the next day.

It was about three in the afternoon and I was sitting there, looking through a calendar featuring North Carolina's flora and fauna
when Jeannette swished by and asked me to take a file up to one of
the lawyers, someone I hadn't met before.

His office was upstairs and at the far end of the building, next to
a line of windows that overlooked the train tracks. It was deserted
in that part, except for an abandoned copy machine and some dusty
boxes of files and a secretary's desk to the side of the door, where I
saw that Caroline, the old lady, was now sitting. She appeared to be
dozing in her chair, the same prairie dress bunched up around her
neck, her head lolling to the side. I crept past and knocked. No answer. I knocked a little louder.

I was about to walk away when something stopped me. I stood
and looked at Caroline and the crumpled way she was sitting. Her
head was lying back against the chair. Her mouth was open. She
was positioned like a rag doll that had been thrown from across
the room and happened to land that way—one hand resting in her
lap, the other dangling down by her side. Her legs were lolling open
under her dress. She looked deflated, inanimate. My eyes rested
on her chest, searching, I realized, for the rise and fall of breath. I
didn't detect anything and my heart started beating faster and I was
just raising my hand to cover my mouth when there was a voice
behind me.

"She's not dead."

I turned around. It was a man a little taller than me. He had a

ponytail. He looked to be in his forties and had thick brown eyebrows and a forehead that cropped out over the rest of his face.

"Oh, sorry," I said. "I wasn't—"

"No, no, it's fine, I do that a lot, too. Not stare at her," he said
quickly. "But, you know, wonder if she's dead."

I turned back around. I squinted.

"Are you sure she's not?" I said.

"Well, ninety-nine percent."

We stood there.

"Man she's old," I said.

"Yeah." He leaned back on his heels. I felt him look me up and
down. "She's basically a wizard at this point."

We stared for a moment longer.

"She's a great woman," he said, as if he felt bad. "Very wise."

"Sure," I said.

He turned to me, smiled in an open way, and stuck out his hand.
"I'm Elliot."

"I'm Julia," I said.

We turned back.

"Why does she have all those seashells on her desk?" I said, pointing to a chalky pile of shells and rocks.

"It's just . . . Don't ask. Her grandson. I don't know."

"Is she your secretary?"

"Technically, yes."

We continued to stare.

Caroline's eyes snapped open.

"Oh my God," I said.

"I'll just be getting back to my office," Elliot said loudly.

"Elliot Grouse?" I said. "Here." I shoved the folder at him and we quickly walked in opposite directions.

Back down at the front desk, I kept thinking about the interaction. I ate some mints from the mint bowl. I swiveled around. I ripped off a bunch of pages from the flora-and-fauna calendar. Elliot. Elliot Grouse. He had big eyebrows and sleepy eyes and features that sat low on his face. I answered the phone. I searched through the drawers and sharpened all the pencils. It was something about the way he'd looked at me. There was an ingredient there that I needed to isolate.

I finally put my finger on it—it was appreciation. He'd so *appreciatively* appraised me and shaken my hand and smiled. It was a smile that was approving and receptive and open to all possibilities.

I felt jittery. I ate another mint. I turned the floppy, plushy dog over and over in my hands. There was something there, definitely, I thought. Maybe this was going to be easy. Maybe it wouldn't be hard to pour myself into the opening that smile had given because there was a touch of desperation there, too, on his part, I could tell. I thought of his ponytail and his wet appreciation, and the way he looked at me as if I were smeared across the universe and he was dazzled but also wistful.

He reminded me of this couple I'd seen on a tour of the Air and Space Museum in D.C. They both had really long hair and the guy was wearing a cape and holding a stuffed animal, and the woman was wearing a bustier like a medieval wench would wear and they were just drinking each other in the whole time. A sense of hostility and suspicion rose against them from the rest of the group, but I was fascinated. The woman wore dark red lipstick and was overweight but walked as if she had gold coins jingling in her limbs. You could tell they were just really happy to have found each other and they didn't care what anyone thought and there was nothing either of them could do that would be embarrassing in front of the other person.

I bet that's how Elliot would be, too—really accepting. He'd probably lay me down on some special rug in his house and try really hard to assure me that there wasn't anything I could suggest that would be out of bounds. And he'd be so happy that we wouldn't be able to sit at a metal table in a plaza for lunch without him immediately covering my hands with his and looking at me with puppyish gratitude.

But then I didn't see him for a whole week. He just wasn't around as much as the other people in the office, who were always appearing in front of my desk, like frogs rippling the quiet and asking me to do something. "Julia, can you run this up to the titles office on Green Street?" "Julia, do you think you could impose some order on the supply closet?" "Julia, would you mind unwrapping the minicups instead of just stacking the bags next to the cooler?" He never came by, never visited me after that initial encounter. I waited patiently until I finally had an excuse to see him the following Thursday, when I was supposed to water everyone's plants.

I approached his end of the office carrying the heavy, slushing watering can. Caroline was there again, at the desk, wearing more or less the same kind of dress, and awake. She was attempting to shake a snow globe. I didn't have to look closely to know that her efforts weren't producing any action. Her head doddered up and down as she brought the snow globe to the left, then the right, then the left again. I walked up to Elliot's door and knocked. I tried again and still nothing.

I turned around and Caroline was looking at me. "He's not in," she said loudly.

"Okay," I said. I indicated to the watering can. "I just have to—" I turned the knob and pushed.

"Wait—" she said.

I shut the door behind me.

His office. It was dim without the lights on. It felt like a library, everything serene and orderly and muffled. White shelves lined the walls. There was a cup of oversteeped herbal tea on his desk, next to his wireless keyboard. There was a glass paperweight with some pyramids inside it. I walked over to look at one of the pictures on the wall, half noticing that there were no plants in the room except for a little cactus on his desk, which is probably what Caroline had been trying to tell me. It was a large framed poster—a reproduction of a pencil sketch, of a young man, a Native American, sitting on the edge of a wave that had been frozen in time right as it was about to crash. He was dangling his legs over the side, where it was jagged with foam and froth. And then above him, composing the top part of the poster, was a majestic hawk with its wings spread, and in its chest was the moon. Below, it read "Elsu."

I heard the door clicking behind me. I turned around. Elliot.

"Ah," he said, glancing quickly around the room.

"Hi," I said. I held up the watering can. "I was just . . ."

"Oh, sure," he said. He walked to his desk and laid a book down on it. "Well, I only have the one," he said, pointing to the cactus.

He didn't seem pliable like he had when we first met. He looked a little unnerved to see me in there, not exactly filled with unalloyed gratitude.

"Right," I said. "Yeah, I noticed. And I guess it doesn't need any." I held up the can again.

"No," he said.

We stood there. He put his hands on his hips and looked around, closed off.

"I guess it's just nurtured by the winds of time," I said.

He unlocked a little.

I was about to walk out when he said, "Are you a fan?" and nodded at the poster.

"Oh," I said. "No. I don't know."

"*Elsu*," he said. "It's a book. It used to be pretty famous. It's about a young Native American guy who could freeze the ocean. He had this mission where he was supposed to climb the tallest wave so he could see his ancestors in the moon from there. And that hawk was his friend and would always guide him to the biggest storms."

"Oh, okay."

"And so there are lots of great scenes of him walking across the ocean, along all these planes and dunes of water, under the moon, watching whales under the surface and, you know"—he seemed less sure of himself now; he looked down and gingerly touched the top of his desk—"following his internal music and talking to a hawk."

"That's pretty cool," I said, a little too quickly, "to be able to do that."

"Yeah," he said.

"To be able to talk to a hawk," I clarified.

"Right," he readjusted. He walked around his desk and sat down in his chair, more composed. He leaned back and smiled. "So, do you think it would be better to be able to talk to a hawk, or stop time?"

I couldn't tell if he was sort of joking around, or if he really wanted to know. "Talk to a hawk," I said. "Wait, no. Stop time. Obviously."

"Right, because then you could—"

"You could, like, stop time during a tour of the White House, and then go into the Oval Office and rummage around and look in a bunch of secret files."

He smiled. "So that's what you'd do?"

"Well, I mean, that's just the first thing I thought of."

He put his hands behind his head. "I'd do it on a tour of these caves—have you even been to Luray Caverns?"

I shook my head.

"They're these caves in Virginia, like something from another world. I'd stop time on a tour and go and explore them by myself. They're all lit up. It's beautiful. There's even a piano in one part."

"A piano? Really?"

"Or like an organ. Like from a church."

"Do people play it?"

"Well, presumably," he said. "I think they use it for weddings."

"Who would get married in a cave?"

"Well," and then he said, with a little flourish, "dwarves, elves, or any panoply of folkloric beings."

I didn't laugh immediately, and he became embarrassed, and then I laughed too hard to catch up.

He tucked his lips in and shoved forward in his chair, like he really needed to get to work.

"Well," I said, in a blur, "I guess I'll get back to this," and held up my watering can.

"Okay," he said, not looking up.

Back at my desk, I watched a woman in white capri pants walk up the pebble walkway and peer into the office, then decide against something and hurry away. I went over the conversation in my head. I'd definitely misread him when we first met. He was at the same time more confident and more sensitive than I'd thought, with all these levers and pulleys inside that I didn't expect. I thought of the way he touched the top of his desk, and then how he'd leaned back in his chair. At moments he'd seemed almost familiar to me. And there was a warm, humorous sinew to his personality that I liked. I had a sense of what he was interested in, and I needed to come up with more stuff for us to talk about. I thought of the cactus on the windowsill in Viv's kitchen. Maybe I could bring that in and put it on my desk and that would establish some mutual interest. Or, that's stupid. People didn't ask each other about their cactuses.

— *Five* —

It was hot. I watched two construction workers share a cigarette across the street. They were sitting on a concrete barrel surrounded by long grass in front of a gutted building. They were talking and passing the butt back and forth in what seemed like slow motion. I couldn't hear what they were saying because of the sound of the train—a dark roar that shook my teeth in their sockets and shook the storefronts. The two men nodded slowly at each other. Together, they turned their heads to me. The train passed. The bar lifted and I walked across the overgrown tracks.

I was going to meet the "TheMeeksShallInherit" guy from the Internet, whose real name was Bill Meeks, for dinner. We'd finally settled on a time and place after a few days of wrangling, mostly on his end. I figured that in case whatever incipient thing I had going with Elliot Grouse didn't work out, it would probably be good to put some other irons in the fire. Maybe this could just be it, I'd thought, swiveling my hand through a bracelet, looking out my window at the bright field as I got ready. Our e-mails back and forth had had a promisingly chatty, easygoing nature to them that seemed like it would translate to dinner conversation. And people had sex with people they had nice conversations with all the time.

I got to the restaurant a little early. It was a seafood place with small white tiles on the floor and a pleasant, dish-clanging energy. There were napkins standing on plates and it seemed expensive.

I was led to a booth. I sat down and stared at the menu and rummaged through my bag. I found a lint-covered packet of gum I didn't know I had and started chewing a piece. There was a commotion toward the front. I looked up and saw everyone's head turned toward a man with a large scruffy dog. They were barreling through the restaurant. A couple of waiters looked at each other, exasperated, and one tried to intercept them. I turned back to the menu and flipped through it a little more, but then I realized they were headed in my direction. I looked up. It was Bill Meeks. He was in front of me, the dog was panting frantically and trying to jump up. Bill got down on his knees and hugged him. "This is Henry," he said. "Good boy, good boy."

I leaned back. I had no idea what to do. Everything was noisily bobbing right there. "Hi," I said.

Something was off. Not just because he'd brought a dog into the restaurant. He looked different. He was older than his online photo by at least ten years. His face seemed to have sunken in and bulged out at the sides.

"I just wanted you to meet him. Say hi, Henry!" He held up the dog's paw. I waved tentatively. "Okay, I'll be right back," he said.

He walked out of the restaurant with the dog and disappeared from view. I sat there, embarrassed, aware that people were still looking my way, and stared at the menu.

He returned and sat down in front of me. He acted like we were still in the wake of some previous joke or bout of laughter. "I know, I know," he said, a little out of breath. "He's the best, he's a character. So." He looked at me. "What are we having?" He picked up the menu.

He was wearing creased khaki pants, a T-shirt that had a city-scape on it and read "St. Louis," and a navy blue blazer that was too small. On one of his fingers was a large, bulging, golden class ring. He looked like he'd just come off a three-day bender on a friend's yacht. He was fidgeting under the table, shaking his knee up and down. He glanced up and smiled at me in a distracted way and went back to the menu. He shifted in his seat, sat forward, sat back. He cracked his knuckles, coughed a kind of preliminary cough. He craned around and looked toward the front of the restaurant. He leaned forward and picked up a saltshaker and scrutinized it and put it down.

"He's great," I said. "Henry. He seems really friendly."

"Oh yeah, he's the best. The best." He rubbed his hands together, raked them through his hair.

"You been here before?" he said.

"No," I said. "Are you from"—I pointed at his shirt—"St. Louis?"

"What? No," he said. "But I've heard it's the greatest. Just the greatest."

"Yeah," I said.

"You've been there?" he said.

"St. Louis? No. But, yeah, I've heard it's pretty good. It's got that arch."

"What?"

"That arch?" I pointed to his shirt. "That arch there. The arch?"

"Ah," he said, smiling, vaguely perplexed.

We went back to the menus. The waitress came and we ordered drinks. I ordered wine and he ordered beer.

"I guess we're not challenging any gender conventions," I said.

"What do you mean?"

"I mean with our drink orders."

"Oh, right." He regarded me briefly with what seemed like a touch of annoyance. He shook his head quickly as if trying to straighten everything out.

"So, Julia," he said, once our drinks were delivered. "Julia Green-field."

I nodded. Took a sip of my wine.

"Tell me about yourself," he said. "Tell me three things. That's right—I went to a job interview the other day. The guy said, 'Tell me three things about yourself, or, describe yourself in three words!' I said"—he started counting things off with his fingers—"I'm loyal, I'm a people person, I get along with just about anyone, that's true, I'm really friendly, and I'm also punctual. I could have punched myself. 'Punctual'? What a knucklehead."

"Well, also you said four things," I said.

"What?"

"Loyal, a people person, friendly, punctual."

I had meant to say it in a joking way.

"I guess you're right," he said.

He looked bleakly out the window. His face had fallen. On the street, a man wearing a sandwich board with stars and stripes on it walked by. Bill played with the sodden paper coaster under his water. This was terrible. How had this happened? Why had I said that? What was going on here?

The waiter came and took our orders.

I had to get back—I sensed there was some sunny territory just above us on which we could connect. I had to change my whole bearing, ramp it up to match him.

"I've been asked that, too," I said, laughing. "On a job interview. It's so stupid. No one tells the truth. I mean, what are you supposed to say, 'I'm obsessed with spreadsheets!'"

"My mother," he said. "She's a great lady, a really great lady. But she's a handful. I was— We were at her house, trying to fit a sofa through the doorway. It's at one of the new places, out there up Route 29? Really nice, and she keeps saying, 'It fit through the breezeway at Delmarva! It fit through the breezeway at Delmarva!' And there we are, with this huge green sofa, stuck in the door. I was like, 'Mom!'" He put his hands up in a helpless gesture. "'Mom! What am I?'" He shook his head in disbelief. "'What am I?'"

He looked at me for a reaction. I cleared my throat. "Yeah," I said. "So, are you close with your mother?"

"Yeah," he said glumly. "I would say so."

Next to us were a couple of lawyer types, working on a case, fountain pens poised, the lady's hair tied back in a classy French twist. I watched as she flung her head back and laughed, and the man looked hungrily at her neck.

"Does she live around here?" I asked. "Your mom?"

"Emmitsville."

"Oh, that's not far from where I'm staying, with my aunt."

"You live in Emmitsville?" he said.

"Well, between here and there."

"Isn't that where the new drive-in theater is?" He was flipping a coaster over and over in his hand.

"Oh, really?" I said. "That would be cool. I haven't heard of it."

We picked over a few more topics of regional interest and then our food came. I kept trying to decide if he was handsome or not. He had dark blond hair that was swept back with a fair amount of gel, and there was something about him that suggested a high-school heartthrob gone out to seed, or a golden young actor past his prime. He was good-looking, I decided, but it was also as if the surface of his face had become unmoored and drifted ever so slightly off-center. Still, he had a kind of antic warmth. I imagined us in a cabin, or a room with wood paneling, in bed, and he's propped up on his elbow and walking his fingers up my chest. Then he maniacally kicks off the sheets and decides to make a crazy omelet. Then he's goofing around in the kitchen with a skillet on his head and we're both in stitches. I was starting to be able to see it, the way it would be with him, everything hilarious and spontaneous and slightly unhinged.

With the arrival of our second drink, we started talking about a man in town who we had both encountered, who may or may not have been homeless, and who sat on a pail on the downtown thoroughfare and played the same tuneless melody on his harmonica day in and day out. The sound had become synonymous with that area.

"Every freaking day!" said Bill.

"I know," I said. "He's like some background extra in a computer game."

"It would be one thing if he knew how to play the thing."

"It's terrible!"

"And look"—he put his hands up in a defensive gesture—"I like zydeco."

I laughed. "Oh, so that's what it is?"

"Yes," he said, with an air of authority, his eyes suddenly stern. "It's zydeco."

"Okay."

"But this is getting out of hand. Learn a different tune!"

It was all-encompassing, when he was animated—his flashing eyes, his large face and golden hair.

We looked at each other, a little too pleased by this burst of agreement.

"Let's get out of here," he said, his eyes gleaming.

"Now?" I said. "But what about . . . We have to pay."

"Ah." He produced a crumpled ten-dollar bill and threw it on the table. "Here," he said, "you talk to the waiter, I'll go get Henry." And before I knew it, he was walking out of the restaurant.

I sat there for a second, taking this all in. I found him outside. But before I could tell him he owed me thirty dollars, Henry yanked him away. "Come on!" he said.

Then we were swinging down the street, jerked along by the dog, who frantically ran around and made hairpin turns. I almost had to run to keep up with them. Bill kept laughing and looking back at me appreciatively. Was this going really well and I just didn't know it? Was he on something? Were we having a great time? I tried to align myself with just that, that the recent turn of events on our date had exhibited the kind of spontaneity usually associated with people who were having a lot of fun together and were mutually delighted by the kind of madcap things that were taking place, that just naturally arose from our special chemistry.

I pictured us making out on a ski lift, his face rugged and tan. I saw us in an imports store, and he's playing peekaboo behind an ethnic mask.

We passed a hot dog stand, a yarn store. We walked through a pavilion where some men were setting up chairs for an outdoor concert. "Where are we going?" I said, out of breath, when I caught up with them on a street corner.

"We're almost there," he said.

Finally we ended up at an old carousel, at the end of the historic district of the downtown area. It had golden poles and red and blue and green horses. But the paint was chipping and the whole thing was surrounded by chains. It had obviously been out of commission for some time. A tall building cast a shadow down one half of it.

"Ah, man," he said. "This is so great. Isn't it great?"

"Did you come here as a kid?" I said.

He was kneeling, tying Henry up, and he exploded with laughter.

"Come on," he said, out of breath. He climbed over the chains and got on one of the horses. He started whooping and waving his arm around.

"What are you—"

"What? C'mon!" he yelled.

Henry was barking. I wanted to run away. A woman holding

two white shopping bags walked by; her eyes flitted back and forth between us. She picked up her pace. I climbed over the chains and got up onto the carousel. I hitched my skirt up and hoisted myself onto one of the horses next to him.

"Well," I said. "This is—"

"My friend Trevor?" Bill was looking away from me, toward a redbrick apartment building in the distance. "He's such a cutup, he'll do anything!"

"Yeah?"

"Yeah, we went to Meade Park the other day. You ever been there?"

"I've driven past it."

"We went out there to"—he made a knocking-back-a-bottle drinking gesture—"'relax' yesterday. There were all these little kids. There were rides and stands. It was some kind of festival. So me and Trevor, we go over to that giant chessboard, you know, the one under the tree? And you can haul all the pieces around?"

"I've always wanted to use one of those!" I said.

"So we go over there, and there are all these little kids on it, you know, pushing around the pawns and things?"

"Okay," I said.

"So Trevor goes over there, and he's been drinking from his flask of tequila? So he goes over and he starts talking in a Mexican accent." Bill suppressed a giggle. "He goes, 'What do I do with theeees theeeeng?' And this one kid is like, 'What?' And Trevor picks up the king and goes, 'Theees keeeng, man, what do I do?'"

Bill's eyes were shining. I started chipping a piece of paint off the ear of my horse.

"The kid is all serious. He's looking around, looking at his mom. And she's standing in the corner and she is, I mean, she is mad."

Bill pushed down another gale of laughter. He bit his fist. The sky was turning orange and there were faint musical notes in the distance—an ice-cream truck getting closer. "But the best part, the best part is— Okay, so all the kids have gone back to playing their game, and we're watching from the side. And then just when they start up again, when the same little kid decides to make a move, Trevor, he goes over there and takes the king and runs off with it— everyone is like, 'What?'—and puts it under this, like, canopy, and then he runs back and he's like, 'Checkmate, you little shit!'"

He bursts into helpless laughter.

I laugh, too, drawn along, though I'm not sure what the joke is.

"Checkmate!" Bill says, doubling over again.

"Yeah," I said, giggling. "An age-old chess maneuver, getting drunk and cheating."

"What?" he said.

"What?" I said.

He turned his head away from me, back toward the redbrick apartment building. A plastic bag crawled by in a warm breeze. Somewhere, the ice-cream truck blared and passed us. Bill was now quiet, looking at something in the distance. I wasn't sure what was going on.

"No, it's just"—I tried to laugh—"it's just a funny game strategy."

When he looked back at me, his face was different.

"Why can't— What about you?" he said.

"What?"

An awful petulance had come over his mouth.

He jerked his chin up. "Look at you."

"Me?"

"Yeah, you. Look at you. You're disgusting."

"What?" I was still half smiling.

I looked down. I'd had to hike up my dress to get on the horse, and it had ridden up my legs, but it wasn't showing anything.

"You look desperate."

"Wait—"

"And you know what?" His features were twisted and malicious. "When you eat? Your gums stick out. It's disgusting."

For a moment, all I could do was sit there and stare at him. An elderly couple walked by. One of them was holding a stuffed teddy bear. They looked our way, smiled at us ruefully.

Bill was staring to the side, fuming, his face cold. He shook the pole that went through his horse. "Just like fucking DeeDee," he said.

I slowly started to climb off the horse. I let myself down onto the carousel floor; my skirt fell around my legs.

He shook the pole again. "Just *like* fucking DeeDee. She's this fucking bitch at work," he said.

I stepped off the carousel and picked up my bag. Bill laughed a bitter little laugh. I walked over the chains, as if floating, and then floated silently down the street in the direction of my car.

It wasn't quite dark. Reggae music wafted over from a restaurant where a few people stood on the patio. A man in an overcoat, despite the warm air, stood under a streetlamp and talked to himself. I concentrated on my shoes.

All the way home I tried not to think of anything, but to focus on

the cones of light in front of my car. I didn't want it to drain back
into me. I didn't want to think about what I felt—that I'd stayed and
stayed and stayed, so far past the point when I should have gone
home. I felt smeared with Bill's presence. His drifting, loud, unmoored face floated in front of me. The road was lonely and deserted. A minivan with the lights on inside passed me, someone
jabbing at the ceiling.

Back at Aunt Viv's, the sound of my key in the front door lock
seemed to boom through the night. There were crickets and cur-
rents of honeysuckle in the air. A hot belt of tears formed behind
my eyes.

I was surprised to see a light on in the kitchen. I hesitated at the
stairs, and then wandered down the hallway. Aunt Viv was at the
table, wearing a floor-length nightdress, writing in a leather book
with a newspaper open on the table. Next to her hand was half a
glass of wine.

She looked up and smiled a sleepy smile. "It was too hot in my
studio," she said.

"Oh, that room upstairs?" I said, standing in the kitchen doorway. I almost added, "That you always keep locked?"

She nodded.

"I'm sorry." I walked in and dropped my bag on a seat, trying to
seem casual. I got a glass from the cupboard and filled it with water.
I took a few deep breaths, standing there, looking into the drain.
Then I turned around and leaned against the sink. For the first time
I noticed that the tops of Viv's shoulders were completely red.

She caught me staring. "A bad sunburn," she said, "from when I was a teenager. I fell asleep in the sun. It never came out."

"I didn't know that could happen," I said.

"Me neither," she said.

"It doesn't still hurt, does it?"

"No, no." She pushed down in the book with her pencil, scraped it back and forth a few times as if to sharpen it.

"I'm mapping out my project," she said, "with the plates."

"Oh, okay."

"I want to tell the whole story," she said. "Merlin, the Knights of the Round Table. I'm even going to have a title plate."

"That sounds great."

Maybe it was the intimacy of being up together, or maybe I just didn't feel like being alone after what had happened, but I kept standing there at the sink.

She glanced up and asked me how my evening was with a kindly indifference that made me want to put my head against her shoulder and weep.

"It was—" I was trembling, about to break, but I pulled it together. I exhaled. "It was fine." I laughed a little. "Bad date."

"Oh?" I couldn't tell if Viv was touched or unnerved by this admission, veering, as it was, into more personal territory.

The lacy curtain above the sink fluttered in a warm breeze. How good it felt to be somewhere softly lit, and warm, and private. I felt relieved by all the land, the sheer mileage between me and Bill Meeks.

"Yeah," I said. "The guy was . . . not a nice guy."

"I see," she said, nodding. I could tell she wanted to offer more.

I didn't know anything about Viv's romantic history. I thought I heard that she was involved with someone named Richard a very long time ago, but I couldn't remember the details. I knew she'd never been married. I studied her. She was in her late fifties—but her forehead was smooth as a stone. She looked pretty with her long red hair behind her shoulders and her regal posture, her face calm as a pond. I could see some raggedy old soldier laying his head in her lap.

She dropped her hands to her knees. "Yes," she said. "That can happen." She looked at me, her eyes friendly. "I'm sure you told him off."

"May I?" I said, pointing to a bottle of wine on the counter.

"Of course."

What did she think of me? What would she think if I told her I was a virgin? I wanted to tell her right then, because I was sick of lying about it, sick of pretending to be something I wasn't and contorting myself to cover it up. I opened my mouth, but then I couldn't—I couldn't stand watching her try, in her polite, reserved way, to assemble some kind of sympathy.

I got a wineglass out of a cabinet and walked to the table and took the bottle and poured some and said, "Told him off? Not really. I wish I had. Have you known guys like that? Or men? Who just sort of want to put you down?"

She gave a sort of shrug. "I think so."

"He was strange," I said. "It was like trying to talk to a pinball machine."

This made her laugh. "Well, at least it wasn't boring," she said.

"But he was boring, too."

She looked at me with curiosity.

"I know, it doesn't make any sense."

"It doesn't sound like a very good combination," she said, smiling.

"I still had to be the one to make the conversation go."

"I know what that's like."

"It's horrible, isn't it?" I said. "Having to do all the work?"

She nodded.

"You have to hope something will catch."

"Yes!" she said. "I knew a man like that once. It was at a training session I had to do, at the Piedmont Center. We were partners and had to put together a presentation and spent the whole day together." Viv was talking with a fluidity I wasn't used to, and I realized that she was a little drunk. "He didn't utter a peep the whole time, and so I found myself talking nonsensically about anything and everything. Making preserves." She tossed up her hands. "Airport mosaics."

"It's exhausting!"

She nodded, smiling.

"Have you ever been on a date like that?"

"Sort of," she said. "But I haven't"—she shook her head—"I've never really been with a man." She stole a look at me.

"What?"

"A virgin." She put her hands up, trying to make a joke out of it. "What do they call it?—a maiden aunt."

She studied me and then quickly turned back to her leather book.

Later, when I looked back on that moment, trying to unpack it

and go over it and study the exact grain, I remembered the feeling
of being under a lot of pressure, because what Viv wanted was to
gauge my reaction. I didn't offer her anything. I just stood there,
dumbstruck. She was writing in her book, her brow furrowed, in
what seemed like feigned concentration. I almost came out with
it. I almost said, "Me too!" But what a weird clay that would have
made in the air between us. Where would we have gone with it?
Instead I watched in silence as she took another sip of wine and
then erased something and tore the page and smoothed it out.
There would be times thinking back when I wondered if I'd misinterpreted it. Why would she admit that in such a casual way? Maybe
she didn't care. Maybe she'd reached a sage understanding about
it. But then I would remember how she glanced over—her searching expression after she told me, and I could tell. It factored in. It
factored into everything.

How could this be? I thought, sitting at the wicker desk in my bedroom twenty minutes later, unable to sleep, unable to read, clicking
a pen. We'd both been embarrassed. I'd finally said, trying to be
funny, "Well, you're not missing out on anything." She'd nodded
quickly, everything about her demeanor saying she wanted to get
back to work and be left alone.

I listened to the night sounds outside my window, crickets, a
birdcall. The house became alive with the rush of water—Aunt Viv
in the bathroom, getting ready for bed.

I didn't know whether to laugh or to cry. It could happen. It
did happen. The train could pass, and disappear into the distance.

Everything you'd gathered for the right moment could wither in your arms and spiral away in the wind. It was like looking at someone who'd been in a plane crash, or struck by lightning. Someone who had fallen through a random crack of fate, and why, and how easy actually *was* it for this to happen and could it happen to anyone and how was it possible?

I tried to think of everything I knew about Aunt Viv and about the times we'd spent together when I was a kid. There were the card games. I remembered the soft, cool pads of her fingers pressing onto my arm in the hallway. I pictured her caught in the doorway with a bunch of bags, and a few sleeves of flowers, her face flushed, looking where to put them down; she's searching for her keys, upending a small glass frog on our kitchen counter; a spike of laughter from her—her and my mom, in a room somewhere in the house. There was so much time I didn't know her, so much time between then and now when we'd lost touch, and that whole time she'd been not having sex. All those minutes, hours, days, what had she been doing? What had I been doing? I heard the snap of her long denim skirt in the wind. We're at a park, she's scanning the horizon. There were car wrecks, tornadoes, foreclosures, but what about the disasters that could be visited on a person slowly, incrementally, over the course of decades?

It didn't make any sense. Aunt Viv was nice, pretty normal, relatively attractive. She smelled good and was organized. So she was shy and a little reserved. Plenty of people like that have sex. Maybe she was a lesbian and was all repressed and could just never admit it to herself.

Or maybe there was a scrim of need there, only detectable to men, that threw things off, jounced her out of the right rhythm. Maybe she was *doing* something—there was some quality that over the years had gone unchecked, become more pronounced, because you can't see yourself from the outside—that caused her to stay single. That was when I started looking at Viv as a sort of specimen, when I began observing her with a more exacting eye. I had to know how she'd ended up like that, if there was something inherent there, from the beginning, a rogue mannerism or trait that leveraged her out of all of it.

I sat there scribbling on the edge of a piece of paper with a pencil, until the whole top half was dark and shiny with graphite and the corners curled.

Could it still happen? I could see her with someone, having some late-day romance, all worn and forgiving, like falling into an old baseball glove. And they could hold hands and listen to conch shells and he would be in love with her quiet and efficient ways. They could be like those old couples who didn't expect to find each other but then they did, and they would look at each other knowingly from Adirondack chairs and you know they're just fucking with abandon because they were too old to be insecure and were throwing everything against the wall at this point. I could see it. It was still possible. It had to be.

I knew I was going to do it from the moment I woke up and heard Aunt Viv's car roll down the gravel driveway toward the street, but I still forced myself to take my time eating my cereal that morning. I

glanced at the paper, sat on the already hot porch steps, and looked out toward the road. Without any conviction, I tried to work on my essay, picked up and studied a decorative papier-mâché pitcher that was on the top of the fridge, opened a cabinet in the dark sitting room, and looked at a set of dusty old poetry books. All the while it was welling up inside me—what I was going to do.

There's nothing more quiet than an empty house at midday, a moonscape of chairs and vases. I stood outside Viv's room and pushed the door open and it creaked. I stepped in. Cool, blue-tinted half-light came through the window. It smelled like her. I walked slowly across and looked out onto the front, the gravel driveway winding away.

Her bed was a wooden four-poster, an antique, with an expanse of cream-colored comforter. It was all tidy, airy, pleasant. There was a colorful, tattered oval rug on the floor. I felt that everything was so finely tuned, the strings pulled so tightly to achieve a specific chord of worn comfort, that she would know, immediately, that someone had been in there. But that's ridiculous, I told myself.

On the table next to her bed was a copper vase and inside it were stalks of fake rustic-looking leaves, the kind of cheap thing you get at a craft store. On her bedside table were a decorative candle, a bracelet, and a careworn paperback mystery.

There were framed photos on the wall: a tired-looking couple standing in long grass in front of a shed; another showed three people next to a beat-up blue truck. One was Vivienne, probably a teenager, wearing a denim pantsuit. Her thick hair was tied partially back like a Greek goddess. The person next to her was my father—I hadn't seen many pictures of him at that age, and it's funny seeing the young, open faces of people you only ever knew as adults. And then the third person was another girl, taller and slimmer than Viv but obviously related, and I realized that it must be Ellen, the dead sister. They were all squinting into the distance, their noses making sundial shadows across their faces.

What was I expecting to find? I wasn't sure. A diary, maybe, letters, anything that would give insight into her or her past.

Aunt Viv's dresser was in a sort of feminine disarray, as if she'd been hurriedly searching for something before she left. There were decorative antique bottles. A silver dish contained a tangle of earrings and bracelets and hair bands. Necklaces hung from the mirror—heavy silver and turquoise things I hadn't seen her wear. A snakeskin address book lay open, numbers and streets written in blunt pencil.

I opened one of the drawers to find a stack of neatly folded cotton underwear. Nestled next to it was a scented satchel that smelled of dry spices and cinnamon. Inside the other drawers were socks and nylons and a jewelry box with antique rings in velvet compartments. A long drawer at the bottom that spanned the width of the dresser contained a dusty and mothball-smelling zip-up plastic storage pouch holding some old frilly-looking garments and big gold costume brooches. Tucked in with the clothes was a stack of dusty old postcards, rubber-banded together. I took them out. One was completely black. "Dallas at Night," it read. On the back was faded pen writing of someone named Carrie. "Your 'favorite' city misses you," it read, and then talked about visiting an aquarium.

The phone rang and the sound crashed through the house. I

knocked my wrist on the corner of a pulled-out drawer. Everything was still and quiet again and the call went to voice mail.

Next I went into the bathroom. It looked like it had been re-modeled fairly recently as the faucets were modern silver and the shower was inlaid with sandy-looking tile. There were starfish de-cals on the wall and a seashell-shaped scented plug-in.

I looked quickly through everything. There were hard little Euro-pean soaps under the sink—the kind of thing you get for free at a bed-and-breakfast, all collected and stowed in an orderly way. There was a stiff plastic bag filled with shower caps, a hatbox filled with layers of pastel-colored tissue paper. The medicine cabinet contained scissors in a plastic pouch, spotless nail clippers, Q-tips in a small jar, a stealthy razor in an embarrassingly pink dock type of thing.

There was another scented satchel by the sink, and a glass-doored cabinet above the toilet that held clean hand towels and some toilet paper. It was all so normal, blameless. I closed every-thing and left the room quickly, feeling like I hadn't found anything out and instead had done some kind of unquantifiable, faraway damage to an organ I couldn't see.

"Did you know?" I said to my mom.

"No," she said. "Well, I suspected."

I slammed the car door and stood in a vast, sweltering parking lot. I shielded my eyes from the sun. It was too hot in the car, and it was too hot out here. I needed to find shelter. I was in a gutted shopping center, where I'd seen online that there was a used-book store. All the shopfronts looked dark and closed, and mine was the only car. I walked quickly across the lot toward a bench in the shade under an awning.

I'd just told my mom about the conversation with Viv.

"Well, I mean, do you think she's gay?"

"But I'm not surprised," said my mom, in a musing way, ignoring what I'd just said.

"Why?" I said. "Why aren't you surprised?"

"No, to answer your question, I don't think she's a lesbian. But I suppose anything's possible."

I heard some kind of drone start up over the phone.

"What is that?"

"It's the fan," said my mom. "I just turned it on."

"How's Costa Rica?" I said. "What's it like?"

"So far it's very nice," she said in a patient tone, the tone she used when she was trying to sort through things in an incremental manner. One of my memories, the thing that I often flashed to when I thought of my mom, was her sitting at our kitchen table in Texas, moving pieces of macaroni across the surface to indicate the steps in some process she was about to enact to remedy a problem at work. "We'll call the warehouse. *Then* we'll speak to Harry Comstock. *Then* we'll think about the price point."

Across the parking lot in the distance, a man walked in a hunched manner. He was wearing a neon crossing guard jacket. I couldn't tell where he had come from or where he was going.

"How's Dad? What's he doing?"

"Your father went to see if they have electric converters for his laptop. He didn't bring the right kind of thing."

"Sounds like you guys are having a blast."

"Actually a wonderful man took us up a mountain the other day. At the end of it he gave us a small doll made out of beads. But I didn't have anywhere to put it. I didn't have a pocket."

"But about Aunt Viv," I said, focusing in. "Why aren't you surprised that she's a virgin?"

My mom sighed. "I guess it's because I never knew of her going out with anyone."

"Well, I mean, what was she like when she was younger? When you knew her?"

I got up and started walking, keeping in the shady part, toward one end of the shopping center, where some hanging letters read "ook World."

"She was sort of dreamy, Vivienne. Removed."

"I don't think of her as being that way. I think of her as being straightforward."

"She could be like that, too. She was both."

"What else?" I said, frustrated. "What else do you remember?"

"Well." I heard a rattling sound on the other end. Pills in a bottle. "This damn thing. What?" she said.

"Vivienne," I said. "What was she *like*?"

"I don't know. She's my sister-in-law. She's— We always got along."

"That's not what I'm asking."

"She could be a bit of a know-it-all."

"Okay."

I stared through the glass into the bookstore. It was obviously closed and had been shut down for some time. Overturned cardboard boxes spilled paperbacks across the floor. Still, I tried the handle. It was locked. I turned around.

"Well, so," I said, "what do you mean?"

In the distance, the man in the crossing guard jacket came into my sights again. He walked into some trees. Where is he going? I wondered.

"Well, she could never be wrong about something," said my mom. "I remember once she decided to do a sort of project where she splattered paint across a blouse, you know, to get that effect? To wear it that way?"

"I guess."

"And it looked, predictably, like a disaster."

"Okay."

"But she'd made a big deal out of the fact that she was going to do it. So she wore it anyway, as if challenging us to say something. I don't know why I remember that. It was so long ago."

"But I mean do you think that's why? She was never with anyone? Because she was that way?"

"She got really into glassblowing for a while," said my mom, ignoring me. "It was a real phase."

"What does that have to do with anything?"

"Well, you *asked*."

More pills rattling.

"I know but . . ."

We were both quiet for a little while.

"I'm asking you *why*. *Why* do you think she's a virgin? If you had to say, if you had to make a guess. I mean, don't you think it's strange?"

"Of course I do."

"Well, so, what's your theory? There has to be something. Something you secretly think."

That's what I wanted. The thing my mother gathered or suspected even if she'd never say. It was like her old friend Joanne, who was always single and really involved in community theater. She would come over with a wooden rattle and be like, "I made this!" and then laugh in a spiky, outrageous way and went to great pains to make sure you knew that she saw the fun in everything, which made it really stressful to be around her, and you got the sense that's why she was never with anyone, but it's not like you could *tell* her that.

My mom sighed. "Well, like I said. She could be quite shy."

"But shy people are in relationships all the time," I said.

"I know that," she said vaguely.

It was going to be one of these things, like the Kennedy assassination, or Amelia Earhart, the earth swallowing up the truth, the last threads of it degraded and eroded by time until there wasn't even a starting point from where to begin looking. And maybe that's what it was like with Viv, maybe there was an unidentifiable line she crossed, a wire she tripped, somewhere deep in her life, that caused her to be a virgin, and maybe she'd had a sense of it at the time in some locked-up place but hadn't acknowledged it, and I would never know what that place was, or what had caused it. I would never know when the switchover came, or what that atmosphere was like to foster it and therefore what to avoid, how to step around it.

A plane flew by overhead. I squinted up.

"It is strange," said my mom, after a moment. "But so is Niagara Falls and I don't sit there and twist myself into a pretzel trying to figure out how it got to be that way."

My first kiss was with a girl, Marianne Wallace. We were ten. She wore red lipstick and seemed to be always tossing her sexuality around, although maybe you can't call it that at that age. She was always pulling down her underwear for someone's brother or asking people to hypnotize her. One afternoon I was over at her house and we were looking at one of her dad's heavy old *World Books*, at the same section we always looked at, which were several transparent pages with different parts of human anatomy on them, so that when you laid them on top of one another they would layer, first with the skeleton, then the muscle, then the organs, then the whole naked body. We were flipping back to begin again when she pushed me to the side and shoved her tongue into my mouth. All I could think was that it was like the arm of a starfish.

In high school there was Eddie, and then in college, after I'd quit swimming, there was a guy named Tim Palover. It was senior year and we'd been partnered up for a presentation in our history lab, and so had to meet up at the library several times. He worked for his dad's moving company and had a thick neck and a sweet, concerned face. He would slowly run his fingers along the books, looking for a specific one, and I liked the way he hovered over everything in a heavy, gentle way. After building up my courage, I asked him out one day, but it turned out that the pleasant, deliberate way we'd had when working together didn't carry over into conversation very well. We sat at a taco place, looking in different directions. I slurped loudly on my soda to fill the silence.

We still ended up going back to his apartment—he lived off campus—and getting stoned and sitting on his sofa. For lack of anything else to do, we silently watched his roommate play a bass-fishing video game where he flung his arm back and forth, to cast the virtual line, with increasing hysteria, until he threw the controller down on the floor and stomped away.

Tim and I looked at each other. We started making out. I'm here, I thought. I'm doing this. It was the middle of the afternoon. I was high, wonky. Sun filtered through a Tibetan scarf tacked to a window. I could tell he wanted to go all the way, that he would do that, and I hardly had to do any paddling to keep it going. He put his hand down my pants and started a rhythmic motion. I liked how he smelled, and the pleasant sensation of his weight on top of me, but this didn't feel good. It reminded me of someone sanding the last drop of varnish off a banister. I tried to want it, to align myself with the grid of pain and pleasure you see on people's faces in porn. His head was now on my chest. He kept doggedly at it. I opened my eyes and looked at the jerking aquamarine waves on the TV, the video game stuck on the menu screen.

He got up abruptly and when he came back with a condom something had changed in me. He could tell. It all fizzled. I gave him a hand job, my first one, and we both had the grim determina-

tion of trying to start a fire in plummeting temperatures. Anything
to save the afternoon. He finally came, and we watched TV for another hour, and then I left.

I still wasn't too worried about it, though, because I had Grace.
We'd become friends quickly after meeting while waiting in line at
the registrar's office and had roomed together ever since. At the
time she had shoulder-length, stick-straight brown hair that sliced
along the tops of her shoulders, and a faint mustache, and she wore
heavy charm bracelets. She was from Pennsylvania, and we had lots
of grave conversations about our pasts. She told me about her
golden brother with whom she'd had a rivalry and who may or may
not have tried to murder their cousin. I told her my biggest secret at
the time, which was that I was pretty sure our neighbor in San Antonio, old Mrs. Penman, was selling Oxycontin to the Mexican construction workers who waited at the bus stop on our street. We sat
in our tiny room, feet up against the minifridge, or spread out on
the hot benches in the rock garden outside the residence hall, or in
the dusty bean bags in the un-renovated part of the library. It came
out pretty soon that we were both virgins, and I clutched this shared
fact. I pulled our friendship over me like a quilt, secure in the knowledge that I wasn't the only one. I was more or less normal. Look at
Grace. I mean, yes, she had a faint mustache and sometimes de-
tached the charms from her bracelet and put them in her mouth
while you were talking to her and her eyes would float around in a
disembodied way, but still.

Then later that year, a guy came out of nowhere and introduced
himself to her on the street. The way she told it, she was walking

from the dining hall to the library, and he was on a bike and was suddenly in front of her. He had a stormy expression on his face, but later it turned out that he was just nervous. He had sharp cheekbones and a buzz cut. He'd been in her chemistry class but there were like a hundred students in the same lecture, so she hadn't noticed him. He wanted to know if she'd like to go on a walk or have coffee sometime, and she did, and they started seeing each other.

It wasn't long before one afternoon I noticed that she was looser in her movements. She laughed with an authority I'd never heard in her before, flung her head back with comfortable abandon. It was like she was welling in being herself. We'd be talking and I could tell her mind was elsewhere, thinking rich, faraway thoughts. She seemed more contained, and more spread out at the same time. An internal shift had taken place and I knew, crestfallen, what had happened.

She confessed it to me one afternoon in the library. The mixture of hesitation and guilt with which she told me only confirmed the direness of my situation. I remember how much I wanted what she had. We were the same two people. Our cells hadn't changed. We were both sitting at the same circular table, at this point in time, in Arizona, like we always did, but now instead of being in it together it felt like we were two separate rotating plates in a rare moment of syncopation and would soon wheel away from each other. And that's pretty much what happened. Sophomore year she moved in with her boyfriend.

It was then that I looked around and started to sense that something I'd previously thought was a given did not seem like such a sure thing anymore. It made talking to guys way more complicated. It was like when an appliance that's been humming along stops working, and you take it apart and realize you don't know how all the parts function or how it ever worked in the first place.

I discovered that I had a haughty way about me. It was something I'd picked up as a kid and never been able to shake—straight blond hair, broad, pointy shoulders, and an aloof manner that I was on some level aware of and yet completely unsure how to dismantle.

After college, I thought moving somewhere completely different would change things, would change me, that I would be shunted into a different humming world with new opportunities and friends and possibilities. I would get a knack for it, like I had with swimming. I'd find the right instincts. I pictured myself in an oval of sunlight on the street outside Arlington Cemetery, the smell of wet leaves, and a different grain to my life. Instead I found myself in a sterile, prefabricated housing complex with no friends. I hadn't realized how much the infrastructure of swimming and college had made it easy to meet people. If I wanted to do so now, I had to crank my life in a way that didn't feel natural—Internet dating or having difficult conversations at bars where you're holding yourself still to talk to someone but the rest of you is floating around the room like a potion. Or, I went to a cooking class for singles once, and everyone there was astoundingly wrong: the stocky man with darting eyes who kept adjusting his belt buckle and mentioning his new duplex, the Canadian guy with womanly hips who disgorged his divorce story after two seconds of conversation.

And then I'd started to feel something I'd only glimpsed as a teenager, when it had been much easier to disregard—actual, corrosive, adult loneliness; a crystalline, desolate feeling of abandonment. Did other people feel this way? I hadn't thought it would be like this when I was a kid.

It sat in me like a jumble of luggage I couldn't put right, no matter how I rearranged it. Everyone else's happiness seemed like a personal affront. I'd walk down the street, shivering in the shocking East Coast cold, and my insides would grind as I watched a couple leaning against the wall, pawing at a manila envelope together and laughing as they shook out its contents. What winds were pushing them and why weren't they pushing me? How did they get lives with all the proper moving parts? I'd study a girl sitting across from her boyfriend at a lazy brunch restaurant, her face blooming, her hair mussed, perfectly nestled in her life, and it seemed impossible, totally out of the question, that that could ever be me. And there was no amount of practicing or trials or laps, no strengthening program to make it better. That helplessness added to my anger. This is a strain of it, I thought, that no one tells you about, this is a strain of being an adult. Desperation seeps into your bones as you lie alone in bed at night, wide-awake.

On my way home from some lackluster night out in D.C. with Jessica, passing lonely newsstands and fogged-up restaurants, and groups of friends jostling one another as they walked down the street, one question would blare in my mind: If things had been slightly different, if certain turns had been taken, could it just as easily have been another way?

— Six —

Elliot Grouse leaned back in his chair. His hand was slung over a paperweight. His desk was covered in papers. There was a completely different atmosphere to his office today—strewn manila envelopes, crumpled pages on the floor. There were cups of old oversteeped tea on the shelves. It looked like he'd been working on something nonstop for days. I shifted my weight from one leg to the other. He was on the phone.

"It's just a swipe card," he said. "A swipe card. A *swipe card*. Mom? We'll get it figured out, okay? I'll call them tomorrow. I gotta go. I'm at work. I gotta go. Okay, Mom?"

I wondered when Elliot ever took the hair out of his ponytail, and if he only did it when he really wanted to relax. I wondered if it melted over his shoulders when he did, and if he would be shirtless, standing in front of the fridge in the middle of the night, or sitting on his bed, staring at his laptop, his hair draped over his back, and he's cupping his chin in this way I'd seen him do, his eyes swimming with sleep.

"I'm getting off the phone now. Joe Cutty," he said. "Yes, Mom, it's still Joe Cutty, and I'll call him tomorrow. Yes. I'm going now. I'm going now, Mom, bye."

He put it down. "Julia," he said, looking at me with a hassled smile. "To what do I owe the pleasure?" And then, before I could say anything, he pointed to my hand. "What's that?"

I was holding a gift I'd gotten for him at a store that sold healing crystals and menstrual calendars and homemade soup spices that I happened to pass one afternoon downtown. It was a transparent disk filled with layers of different-colored sand on a small plastic platform so you could put it on your desk. It was his birthday—which I knew because Jeannette had invited the whole office to cake later—and I'd planned to give it to him in a casual way, like an afterthought, no big deal. It was meant to strike a balance: to encourage him if he was interested in me but not seem too pushy. I hadn't seen him too many times since our last conversation. He'd stopped by my desk once, as if to say something to me, but I'd been on the phone.

"It's for you," I said. I held it out. "For your birthday."

"Really?" he said.

I handed it over. It was wrapped in many layers of tissue paper with mystical glitter in it.

He started unwrapping it.

"You really didn't have to . . ."

He continued unwrapping it.

"The anticipation is killing me," he said.

Finally, he withdrew the sand disk. "Look at that." He held it up. "Are you supposed to shake it?"

"No!" I said. "Well, you can. If you want to. That's up to you. But I don't think you're supposed to."

He slowly lowered it with a perplexed smile and then looked at me, and in the short silence that followed I'm pretty sure it became

clear to both of us that any leverage I'd had by being more con-
ventionally attractive had just been canceled out by this naked and
unasked-for gesture, as well as the fact that the sand disk was, I now
realized, a complete piece of crap that could even be considered
faintly insulting. I watched, with mounting unease, as he registered
all of this and started to form a response that would probably have
attempted to politely paper over the whole thing, but then, instead,
his face became alert and he looked behind me.

"Grousey Grouse," said James Kramer, walking into the office.
"Grousey Grouse Grouse."

James Kramer was the head partner, and when we'd met I'd
immediately disliked him. He was a big, rotund man, white-haired
and jowly, who steamrolled everybody with a loud, aggressive good
cheer. He was the kind of older man who seemed to take it as a
challenge when a woman sustained eye contact with him or coun-
tered him in any way.

"James, hello," said Elliot, putting on a pleasant smile.

"Just wanted to pop in and say a quick happy birthday," said
Kramer, "because I won't be able to make it to Jeannette's little get-
together."

"Ah, got it," said Elliot. "Well, thanks."

James leaned back, his eyes ran over us, assessing. It seemed like
he was going to leave but then he said to Elliot, "How are the little
green men? Are they gathering?"

"Ha-ha," said Elliot. "No, I don't think so."

"Have they started a conference? Are they going to invite you?"
James's eyes flitted over to me with a mean sparkle.

"No," said Elliot, smiling thinly. "I don't think so, not yet."

"Are they gonna"—James made a phone gesture with his hand—"are they gonna phone home?"

"Probably not."

"Well, you'll let me know if they do," said Kramer loudly.

"You know I will," said Elliot.

"You know I want you to," said Kramer, pointing a folder at Elliot, walking backward out of the room. I looked quickly back and forth between them.

"Will do," said Elliot.

"Happy birthday!" yelled Kramer as he walked away from the office.

Elliot glanced at me, shook his head, and started straightening the papers on his desk.

"What was that all about?" I said.

I could tell the interaction had been unpleasant for Elliot, but a part of me was glad it had short-circuited the awkwardness of the previous few minutes and put us back on regular footing.

"It's nothing." He sighed. "It's . . ." He scratched the back of his head. "I made the mistake a couple years ago of telling the guys about this thing—we were just making small talk—this project I was interested in."

"Oh yeah?"

"Yeah." He squinted at me, gauging my actual interest. "It's this thing out of SETI." He put down a pen and leaned back. "They—this started years ago—but they started releasing data they were collecting from a radio telescope in California, where they're sort of sifting for signals from distant technologies, or other civilizations."

"Oh, cool," I said. "UFOs?"

"Yup," he said, "well, exactly. And for the first time they've made all of this data available to the public—you just have to download a program—because they figure a human brain is actually better than a computer algorithm at detecting whether something is just interference from our world, or an actual message from, you know, from outside."

"Got it. Wow," I said.

"So yeah," he said, "and anyone can participate."

"That's pretty cool."

"I just like the idea that you, me, or any old person could identify the first signal like that—what would essentially be the biggest discovery of humankind."

"How much data is there?"

He slowly exhaled. "It would be a needle in a haystack," he said. "A million times that." He smiled. "Are we alone?" he said. "That's the question."

"Yes," I said. "That is the ultimate question."

We made some uncomfortable eye contact. I started blushing.

"Anyway." He shifted in his seat. "Thanks again for the . . ." And he held up the sand disk.

"You're welcome," I said. I hesitated. I wanted to keep standing there. "See you at the thingy later."

"Sounds great," he said, and watched as I turned around and left.

About forty minutes later we all gathered in the kitchen, a fluorescent-lit area that smelled faintly of rotting banana. Jeannette was elaborately cutting the cake she'd made, hustling around the table and moving things back and forth. I was talking to Allison by the refrigerator, but all I could do was glance over at Elliot. This was the first time I'd seen him in a social setting, interacting with other people. He was talking to Ed Branch, his hands under his armpits and leaning forward as if he was really hunkered down in thought.

"My college roommate was from there," Allison was saying. "Where did you go to high school?"

"Wilson," I said. I watched Elliot absentmindedly take a bottle of seltzer from the table and twist off the top. His eyes wandered over to me for a second. I thought about what he did when he got home. If he loosened his tie and untucked his shirt and walked around like that. Maybe that was when he took his hair down. I wondered if he sometimes absentmindedly tossed a grape into the air and then craned his neck back to catch it in his mouth, exposing his Adam's apple.

". . . outside of Plano," said Allison, "but it was more like a lodge than a hotel."

"Uh-huh."

He was still nodding slowly and considering what Ed was saying. Did he pull his cheek taut when he was shaving like men did in movies? And then did he wolfishly towel off the rest of the shaving cream?

Now Jeannette was with us. "Cute haircut," said Allison.

"Thank you, thank you," said Jeannette. "I went to that place Reflections?"

"Oh, just around the corner?" said Allison.

"Yup. I told them—'I wanna look like I have a lot of *fun*.'"

Allison smiled.

Every guy has a different way about him, I thought. Like this guy

Michael Turner, from elementary school. He'd had a serious manner, almost like he knew about some catastrophe that was going to happen in the future and was always staring ahead at it with a troubled expression, like the burden of this responsibility was too much. Eddie had been friendly, with his soft brown eyes, and a footforward, confident way about him that assumed everything was going to line up, and perhaps it was this quality about him that caused things to do so. Then there was someone like Kramer, who was rigid beneath all his forced jocularity. He was probably a tyrant to his wife, though maybe not in any way that was technically illegal, and took everything for himself. That was the type of guy he was—he got out in the front and took everything. What would it be like to be with Elliot? He wouldn't be a tyrant, not in big ways or small ways. I pictured him leaning back in his chair—world-weary but game. He'd look at you with knowing warmth. You'd maybe be at a gas station, in the middle of nowhere, run ragged and tired from driving, and you'd be paying for something at a cash register and you'd feel Elliot's gaze on your back like a soft rain.

Wes came in with Caroline. We all watched uncomfortably as he helped her into a chair, her dress riding up against his arm. When she was finally positioned, she looked around angrily as if the whole world itched.

Jeannette was usually really good at putting people at ease with a salty and hilarious remark, but even her powers were no match for the silence that descended on the kitchen after we sang "Happy Birthday," and Elliot said, politely, "Thank you," and smiled at everyone impersonally, and all the activity of handing out pieces of cake was finished.

The fridge stopped humming. Ed coughed. I started picking at a sticker on the side of the microwave. Elliot furrowed his brow at his plate.

"That's a great platter," Allison finally said, referring to the plate the cake was on, which was shaped like a large sunflower.

"Thanks, hon," said Jeannette. "Just, Elson's Crafts, down on Comstock Road."

I'd been picturing the cave piano a lot, since I'd had that conversation with Elliot. He wiped his mouth with the back of his hand, nodded at Ed. I wondered what it would be like to be there with him—where everything was absolutely still, and absolutely quiet, and there was a pond with the surface like a mirror. A cave was the most inside you could be, the most private place. Maybe it would be completely dark, like I couldn't even see my hand in front of my face. I'd wave my arms around and touch his chest, that place where his work shirts fell in a relaxed way. I'd stumble over there and into him and against the weight of his body.

I was thinking these cave thoughts, and eating my cake, when Ed, motioning with his fork, said to Elliot, "How's that pretty wife of yours? You all still out there in Callan Mills?"

Elliot quickly looked at me. "Fine, yes," he said, turning to Ed.

I stopped chewing.

"That's been a good investment for you all?" said Ed.

"Sure, yeah," said Elliot.

I looked at his left hand. He was wearing a ring.

"Nice area," said Ed. "Looks like a great place to raise kids."

How had I not noticed it? Elliot cleared his throat. "Yes," he said, a little louder, committing himself to the conversation. The finest strings of discomfort pulled in his face. "It is. It's got a great pool, and it's close to a lot of hiking trails."

"Is Devon still out there at the Raleigh aquarium?" said Jeannette.

"She is," said Elliot, glancing over at me again with a scattered expression. "She's still program director. They're keeping her busy."

"I've been meaning to take you up on that free pass," she said. "Take the grandkids. See that new, what is it—y'all got a new manatee over there?"

"Yeah, no, it's a hammerhead," said Elliot. "They have a hammerhead shark now."

"I wonder if those get depressed," said Allison.

We all speculated on that for a little while, and then the group broke up into separate conversations. I tried to concentrate on my plate and arrange myself in a normal way. I spoke to Allison a little more about where she grew up, and me and her and Jeannette commented on the new sandwich place a few streets over, and whether we'd been there or not. Out of the corner of my eye I saw Elliot put his plate in the trash and check his watch and walk out of the room. I could feel him glance over at me as he did so, but I kept my head turned toward Allison.

People dispersed and I helped Jeannette clean up. I don't think anyone noticed that anything was wrong with me, except for Caroline, who was sitting there, and gumming her third piece of cake, and staring right at me, and I could swear the old bitch knew exactly what was going on.

"So how's it all going?"

It was later that day, after work. I was standing in a park and talking to Grace.

"Really, really good!" I said.

I hadn't felt like going back to Viv's yet, so I'd decided to go for a walk. In the middle of a wide, bright stretch of grass was a scratched-up metal sculpture, a dragon's tail coming out of the ground, about knee-high. I sat down on a bench close by.

"It's really hot here," I said. "Sometimes I wish I could unbutton my skin and take it off."

"It's hot here, too," she said. "We get these heat-sick little kids and they're just over it."

I missed Grace. I missed her faint Southern accent and her languorous manner. She was just bobbing along in her life in her fully formed way, and every time she had a problem or needed to talk something out, I wanted to tell her that she was going to be fine, because all she had to do was continue being the way she was and everyone would just naturally give her the benefit of the doubt.

I wanted to tell her about Elliot and how I'd felt when I heard he was married—the stomach-dropping disappointment of it. How I'd sat and methodically unbent all the paper clips in the drawer and then dragged the point of one along the underside of the desk, scratching as hard as I could.

"There's this guy at the place I work," I said.

"Okay."

"I have a crush on him."

"Yeah?" she said hopefully.

She was with a guy named Chad, a nice guy who got stoned a lot and was studying to be a vet. I'd been at their apartment once and I'd studied them—their togetherness—like it was a rare organism. He was tossing a paperweight back and forth while talking to me. He put it down when Grace came up to him and he put his hand on her chest, kind of fit his fingers above her collarbone as if it was a ridge on a rock face and he was going to climb her. I'd thought about that for a long time.

"He has a ponytail."

"Okay."

"But he's handsome. I think so, anyway. He's kind of New Age–y."

"What makes you say that?"

"Well, he has this poster in his office of a mystical Native American children's book. And, I don't know. I just get that sense."

"Well, it's not the end of the world."

"No, but, actually he's married."

"Oh, man." Her voice seesawed. I could feel how genuinely disappointed she was for me.

I got up and started walking along a path. It was humid and the sky had a shiny haze to it.

Grace cleared her throat. "Well," she said, "stay away. There's a lot of drama here about that. The academic curator, she and the associate director of programming and education got involved, but he's married, and his wife is the community relations vice liaison, and she's the ex of our junior associate of senior outreach. You know what? Never mind."

I laughed.

"I was actually looking at our New Age section the other day," she said. "And guess what I found?"

"What?"

"Lucid Dreaming for Beginners."

"No way. Was it the same?"

"Yup. Floating shoe and all."

One of the earliest parallels about our lives Grace and I had discovered was that when we were roughly ten or eleven years old, we had both developed a voracious interest in lucid dreaming, and both went to a lot of trouble to furtively research it, her in her godfather's modern glass home office in Massachusetts, and me in the public library close to my parents' house, where I would spread out a bunch of books of Jaguars to deflect any suspicions. It turned out we had both read the same book, which inexplicably had, among other things, a woman's floating high-heel shoe on the cover.

I thought of those quiet, absorbed hours. "Man," I said, "I miss whiling away the day like that."

"You're telling me," she said. "I've never been so in the moment."

A tired woman pushing a stroller walked by. I passed an old-fashioned-looking water fountain, its base a cascade of concrete flowers.

"I bet she scream-whispers at him," I said. "Elliot's wife. Her name is Devon."

"Devon. Huh."

"I bet they'll be at a cocktail party and she'll get mad and scream-whisper right in his ear."

"It's certainly possible."

"I bet she's always violently applying hand lotion."

"That book did not work," said Grace. "Remember how we'd try to dream of flying or breathing underwater but then we'd end up just dreaming of being random adults?"

"Yeah. We talked about that. Having a superpower. Me and Elliot. Sort of. We talked about what it would be like to stop time. I was just in his office and we got into this conversation and it was really easy and we were just in it."

"I would always dream about being in an airport lounge . . ." Grace trailed off.

I stared at another metal sculpture. It was a hump with spikes on it. Then I realized it was related to the dragon's tail. The whole thing was supposed to be a large sea creature, its body coming out of the surface of the grass in different places.

I looked around. I started walking again.

"Wait, what were you saying?" I said. I wanted to find the head.

"Never mind."

Grace was quiet for a few moments. The sound of cicadas swelled in the air.

"Can I ask you something," she said, "aside from all of this?"

"Yeah."

"What are you going to do?"

"What are *you* going to do?" I said. "What is anyone going to do?"

"I'm asking—where did you see yourself? At this age?"

"Remember that guidance counselor at Arizona?" I said. "With all the stacked-up pudding cups?"

She waited.

"Okay, the way I saw myself at this age? I'm wearing a black leather jacket. I've got a searing expression on my face and my long hair is flowing in the breeze. There's obviously a lot on my mind. Maybe I'm holding a sacred key. Then the camera pulls back, turns out I'm standing in the middle of Stonehenge. It's like, 'Who's that girl? What's she thinking? What is her life?' "

"Okay, well, in case that exact scenario doesn't play out."

"I also saw myself wading through a beautiful lake with purple mountains in the distance."

"You know what I *mean*."

I sighed. "I don't know. I have to get some job, I guess."

I came up to a large marble statue surrounded by shrubs. I stared at the copper plaque without reading it. I wheeled around.

"I have to tell you something," I said.

"What?"

"You're not going to believe it." I laughed a little too hard.

"What is it?"

"Aunt Viv? Who I'm staying with? She's a virgin."

Grace cleared her throat. The pause was complicated and I could feel her choosing her words. She knew, of course she knew, about my situation, and she also knew that whatever she said now would reflect on it.

"Well, that's— How do you know?"

"She told me."

"How? What did she say?"

"She just said it. We were in the kitchen."

"So you guys are getting along?" She was stalling.

"Yeah," I said. "More or less. I think."

Grace was quiet.

"But I mean, how could this happen?" I said. "There must be something wrong with her."

"Not necessarily."

"But it's so strange. Don't you think it's so strange?"

"No," said Grace. "What's strange? I mean, really, in this life? Remember that book? Remember the testimonials? That one lady said she dreamt about crawling through a giant baby's hair. There was that guy with the mustache who said all he wanted to do was not worry and be carried along in a toucan's pouch."

"Yeah." I'd come up to the sea creature's head. It was sticking out of the ground, its neck a long metal trunk. It stared straight ahead with a kind of grimace. Someone had stuck gum in one of its eyes. I felt grateful for Grace. For a moment, I felt like everything was okay. "You're right," I said. "It's a weird world."

— *Seven* —

I stood outside the door of Viv's studio with a heavy copper key in my hand. She'd just left for work, her car crunching the gravel as it ambled down the drive. The day before, while taking a phone message, I'd shaken out a ceramic jar to find a pen. A key fell out, and as soon as it bounced onto the counter I knew what it would unlock.

This was where she holed up often after work, taking a plate of leftovers in, and staying sometimes until late into the night.

I turned the key in the lock and it clicked. I pushed the door open. The first thing I noticed was the cluttered feel and the smell—sweet tea and wood. There was a purplish glow coming from a window that looked out over the side of the house.

Lots of books, framed sheet music on the walls, a flimsy computer desk on one side with knotted nylons underneath next to stacked dusty magazines.

In the middle of the room was a large wooden table. Spread out on top were paint-stained newspapers and mason jars with murky water and brushes inside. I walked around it, studying the plates she was working on. She was creating a meticulous lace-like gold trim around one of them. Another one showed layers of green, with a faint sketch on top, probably meant to be filled in, of a figure on a horse. I paged through a sketchbook where she was trying out ideas and stared at a drawing of a few polar bears swaying to the earth in parachutes.

I went over and sat in the chair across from her computer and laid my hands on the keyboard. A screensaver of a bouncing cube blinked on. I wanted to poke around online—I had a feeling she didn't have the technological prowess to cover her Internet tracks. It was all ordinary, a few gardening websites, some moderate political blogs, her e-mail account. It looked like she was contemplating bidding on old maps at an online antiques auction. I was hoping she had all her passwords set, so that you didn't have to log in, and my fingers were jittery with the possibility of reading her e-mail. But I couldn't; it was closed.

There was a set of drawers next to a sofa and I rummaged through them. They were messy, no rhyme or reason—a few seashells, a cobblestone, fancy stationery on which she'd been practicing her signature, one loopy and casual, another formal and long. There was a tiny Rubik's Cube on a key chain, some leftover antibiotics.

I got up and then sat down on the couch next to a wicker basket holding pincushions—how was it possible for people to acquire so much random stuff? I picked up a box of blank cards with birds on them that was lying there and started to feel a roving, prickly irritation.

The backs of my feet hit something below. I reached down to find a stack of photo albums. From staring at the pictures you would think Aunt Viv's upbringing had been a series of listless county fairs and picnics next to rickety old houses. Generally-dissatisfied-looking people tromped through the albums. But there were some happy photos, too—kids crowded around a sparkler, their faces lit with delight; a group holding hands around a tree, all of them covered in mud.

One photo showed Aunt Viv at probably around eighteen or twenty years old, standing in front of the Alamo. It had been taken in an off moment—she's looking off to the side, her face is troubled as if something had just occurred to her, something deeply worrisome. The hem of her dress is caught in the wind. The background is bright in the sun. I stared at it for a long time, trying to interpret her dark expression. I wanted to ask her about that photograph. What was she thinking about? What had she remembered? What was *wrong* that day?

"It's a blue jay," said Aunt Viv, squinting into the distance. "Bluebirds don't have that crested head, they're songbirds and we don't get them here that often."

We were sitting at a white plastic table on the wraparound porch in the front of the house, eating dinner together for the first time in days. You would think that her admission that night—it had been about a week since then—would have made us closer, but it somehow had the opposite effect. Aunt Viv had started avoiding me. She stayed late at work, e-mailing me to say that she was tied up at the office. When she did come home, she would mostly eat in her study with the door closed. The one Saturday that had intervened she spent gardening, squinting up at me in a distracted way when I walked down the front steps to go somewhere in my car. I didn't mind—I was a little embarrassed, too, but it was getting ridiculous.

So when it happened that we were home at the same time that night, she seemed to embrace it, to want to reset and start over. And that's how we ended up sitting on the porch, at a plastic table she'd dragged out of the garage for something different, eating Chinese food takeout.

I shifted uncomfortably in my seat, stared at a shiny pond of brown sauce on my plate.

"It's pretty," I said. "It's such a bright blue."

"Yes. You can see hummingbirds, too, sometimes, around the honeysuckle at the front door."

I nodded.

"I used to think I would become a bird-watcher," she said. "I got a field guide and everything, but"—a gale of laughter went through her; she brought a napkin up to her mouth to stifle it—"it didn't work out."

Aunt Viv was in a good mood. There was something going on with her. "I got some great news today," she said, confirming my suspicion, glancing at me and then pushing her napkin deep into her lap.

"You did?"

"A man named Pete Wexler called me at work. He said he was from Southern Imports?" She looked at me expectantly.

"The home-goods store?" I said.

"Yes, exactly," she said, nodding.

She went on: "At first I thought it was some kind of mistake. I was in the middle of an admission report and I almost hung up on him. But then he told me he'd seen my website, and that he was going to be at the McCormick show. That that was something he did—he goes to antique shops and art shows and things like that to get ideas. He said he was only going to be in town for the one night, but he was planning to stop by the show, to see if the plates would be appropriate for the store."

"Like to sell them there?" I said, chewing on some noodles.

Viv pushed her lips together in a perplexed, happy way and nodded.

"Wow, that's fantastic, Viv!" I said.

She looked down at her plate, pleased. A bumblebee hovered just above the porch railing.

"So, what would that mean?" I said.

"Well, if I could get them sold there, that would be a real step. A really good step in terms of visibility and distribution. Well, and financially. They sell name-brand things there. It would mean everything. I would have to make it more of a priority." I could tell she had already thought this through a number of times that day. Dreamed about it. "I would have to change my whole way of doing things." She dabbed her lips. "I suppose a long-term goal, and this is something, you know, it's probably too soon to start thinking this way, but that maybe one day I could quit my job."

"Wow," I said.

"Maybe it doesn't seem like a big deal to you."

"Are you kidding?" I said, determined to straighten out any misunderstanding. "Of course it's a big deal. It's a really big deal. It's wonderful!"

I could tell what it meant to her, and I was happy she had this good news, and happy to be happy for her. It was like some internal screw in her had loosened, and all her parts had settled a little with relief and excitement.

"I almost knocked over my cup of coffee at work," she said. "I just couldn't believe it."

"Oh, no!" I said, laughing.

She sighed happily, and looked into the distance, where the sun was just beginning to set, making everything look golden.

She had a kind of domestic finesse that allowed her to do little, old-fashioned things well—make preserves and then label the jars with pleasing cursive, tie perfect bows, bake rustic-looking scones without consulting a recipe. She often had lipstick on her teeth and had a habit of shaking her wrist to get her watch to sit right. These were some of the things I noticed about Aunt Viv.

She hummed beautifully when lost in thought, when gardening or absentmindedly putting things away. She pressed firmly into paper when she wrote and had a disarmingly legible signature. She was plump but not slovenly, and had a way of seeming clean and slapped fresh all the time, as if she'd always just stepped out of the shower. It might have had something to do with her complexion, which blushed easily. Sometimes when entering a room she would cast a cool, queenly gaze around it, and if you didn't know better you could be forgiven for thinking she had an edge of snobbishness to her. I would remember that day at Alice's party, and how she was holding court with her friends, like the popular one at a girls' school, and how imperious she looked.

She read with all the sensuality and absorption of a preteen girl, stocking-footed, sliding down the sofa, completely immersed, her hand foraging on the plate of cheese and crackers next to her like something with a life of its own.

She liked gardening and yanking and patting things down, and you could tell she had grit—like the kind of person who would not freak out on a ship in some survival situation; the kind of person who would sit and watch quietly, taking stock, and only show the chain mail beneath her veneer when an emergency required it. She was a survivor, Aunt Viv. That, I felt, was true, even if sometimes when she laughed it was like the tinkling of simple, pretty light.

She looked more exhausted than a World War One soldier when she got home from work. I watched her once from the top of the stairs when she couldn't see me. She dropped her bag in place and stared at herself in the hallway mirror. She yanked the little scarf off her neck and hung it on a brass hook; shrugged off her linen blazer and hung that up, too, so she was just wearing a white shirt, a circle at the collar revealing her red chest; pulled her earrings off. Things she liked doing included letting her face go all soft when listening to music, clapping her hands to rid them of flour, abruptly changing the radio station, ending a conversation with a quick look away from you, dismissing you, always in the process of dismissal—the hair tie she yanked off her head, the rings she hurriedly swiveled off her fingers, shaking her head to banish an unwanted thought, cleaning out the dirt from under her fingernails with efficient scrapes, shucking away layers to be free; all part of some fastidious, ongoing process—shucking, stripping, cleaning, in preparation for some never-reached point. And then sometimes she would stare into the distance with a bewildered expression and my heart would break a little and I wouldn't know why.

She read everything and knew a lot. It would shoot up now and then like a spit of lava and you would get a sense of the craggy knowledge beneath. "Old Dick Crookback," she said, one afternoon when she got home from work and encountered me on the front porch, reading a book I'd found about Richard the Third. "What?" I said. "That's what they call him," she said, "because of his scoliosis." She looked sad. "He was misunderstood. Such responsibility for an eleven-year-old." She walked into the house.

Once when I came home from work she was in the garden and called me over and she took my wrist and pressed something into my hand. It was an arrowhead. "See," she said. It was black and pointed and hard as all get-out.

I knew that in bed she would be frank and jubilant, if she ever had the chance. She would let her hair down next to a campfire. She would squat in the mornings, outside the tent, to make coffee. She would look at a lover across a campfire with all kinds of mischievous understanding. She would be playful, with a wolf-mother protectiveness, and also a lot of fun.

I could see all these things about her, or so it seemed, and yet none of them told me anything; said anything about why she was in the state she was in, why she hadn't ever been with a man—a more womanly woman seemed to have never existed, and you would agree if you saw her in one of her freshly laundered linen shirts, her chest heaving as she dug for something in the garden, looking up and wiping the sweat from her brow with a gloved wrist, tying her hair up with all this elegant authority. I could picture her waving to someone, a person she loved, in the distance, her alloy of grit and hope shining and shining.

One day in late June, about a month into my stay, I had to pick her up from work. Her car was in the shop and her offices, in a Victorian house a block from downtown, were more or less on my way home. I parked a couple of streets away and walked there and up the steps and through the creaking front door, into a parlor with boxes stacked up everywhere and packing peanuts on the floor. A sweeping staircase led to the second level, where I could see doors with plaques on them.

"Julia?" called Aunt Viv.

I poked my head into a room and there she was, surrounded by drifts of paper and files stacked up around her. Silvery light came through the windows. Her hair streamed down, tenting her shoulders. She was wearing a long green skirt with a pattern of small flowers and a matching blazer, and her cheeks and the rolls on her neck were dappled with red and she looked too healthy and pulsing to be in this half-lit, paper-logged place.

She saw me looking around. She sighed. "It's not usually like this," she said. "We're changing offices around; everything has to be rearranged."

"Oh, okay," I said.

"I'll just be a second."

I wandered across the hall into a golden-lit waiting room. There were fresh flowers on a claw-foot coffee table. A woman at the front desk looked at me irritably. Her hair was scraped back into a hard, shiny bun and she was shoving a folder into her bag. "Can I help you?" she said.

"No," I said. "I'm just waiting for Vivienne."

"Okay," she said, relieved.

"That was Melayna," said Vivienne, as we were walking to my car. A woman with large shopping bags bustled past us.

"What?" I said.

"Melayna," said Viv. "She's our new front-desk person. I'm not sure if it's going to work out."

"Who?" I said. A car blared techno and zoomed by.

"*Melayna,*" she said.

And then there was a man standing in front of us, blocking our way. Even though he was about the same height as Viv, maybe an inch shorter, he appeared to be looking up at her from a great distance. He had gray hair, wispy on the top, and was wearing paint-stained jeans and a faded T-shirt. He looked to be around Viv's age and was smiling a smile that melted his whole face.

"Gordon!" said Viv, surprised.

"I was just coming to find you," he said.

"You were?"

He glanced at me.

"This is my niece, Julia," said Viv.

We shook hands.

"Gordon owns a used- and rare-book shop," she said to me. "Around the corner. On Green Street."

"Cool," I said.

"Just around there," he said, and pointed. I nodded.

There was a pause. Someone down the street opened a jingly door.

"You left your sweater." He held it up.

"Oh, of course," said Viv. "Thank you."

"I did a little more research," he said. "It turns out a friend of mine in San Francisco has the book you're talking about. He's going to send it tomorrow."

"Great! Thank you, Gordon," said Viv.

"Remember"—he drummed his fingers together in a cartoon-ishly nefarious manner—"I have my ways."

Viv burst out laughing.

"Yes," she said, "when it comes to out-of-print biographies of long-dead opera singers, you're the man to see." She had bright-ened and was animated in a way I'd never seen before. She reached up and touched her hair.

"I'll stop at nothing," he said. "I'm a ruthless man."

She laughed through her nose, smiled. "You have to be, in your business," she said.

"All too true," he said.

I looked back and forth quickly between them.

"Do you want to— I just made a fresh pot of coffee." He mo-tioned back toward his store. "You two could join me for a few minutes? I just got some new Audubon prints." But he didn't glance over at me.

"Oh, no," said Viv, laughing, waving her hand. "We have to get home."

"Sure," he said, a little crestfallen.

"Thank you," she said, and held up the sweater. "I'll be in again soon."

And we turned and left him standing there.

In the car, on the way home, I glanced over at Viv. She was looking for something in her purse, taking out receipts and arranging them in her hand.

"He seemed nice," I said.

"I've known him for years," she said, rummaging around. There was still a hint of a smile on her lips.

After a few more moments I got up the nerve to say—even though this wasn't exactly in the vein of our relationship—"I think he likes you."

She went still, and I felt complicated wheels turning inside her.

Then she said, in an amused, taken-aback manner, "Gordon? No."

She went back to looking through her purse.

The way she'd turned down his offer, it was like she hadn't thought it was a real proposition. Her reaction made it seem like he was joking. I thought of the way Gordon's eyes had darted all over her face when they were talking, as if he was trying to map it. What if it had gotten to the point where Viv couldn't see a real possibility when it was in front of her? He was too hesitant to make an actual move because he received all these evasive signals from Viv. And then Viv discounted him because it was never clear if his feelings were real. I drove along feeling disoriented and thinking about what kind of impressions you can give off without knowing, and if it was possible that whole quadrants of your life could be thrown off by this kind of simple misunderstanding.

Here was someone. They rattled like noisemakers when they were next to each other. If they were both too afraid to make a move, someone else was going to have to do it for them.

She was still going through her bag. She collapsed her hands on it and sighed, irritated, it seemed, at having lost something. Then she powered the window down and closed her eyes in the breeze, the way any normal person would.

— *Eight* —

The days shot up, wilted, and dispersed. I discovered a creek, just beyond the line of trees that bordered the back field. It had mossy banks and dank pockets of wet leaves and mosquitoes. It was there that I found a lace glove, sodden and dirty, as if from a tea party a hundred years ago, and a toy dinosaur.

One day I walked along a fence on the west side of the property that bordered a plot of land called Seven Oaks, and I found an overgrown metal bench in a copse of apple trees. On the east side of the property, if you pushed down and walked over some barbed wire, the land tipped just enough so you could see into the neighbor's farm, where a single horse and donkey stood listlessly in the heat most days, which I knew because I went to spy on them a lot, but they never did anything.

One morning there was a dead possum on the stone steps in the back. "Probably ate some poison and waddled there," said Aunt Viv. She got a shovel under it and then dropped it into a trash bag, and the next day someone from the county came to pick it up. Once I saw a hawk dive into the ground and then fly away with a mouse.

Once, walking down the stepping-stones, I startled a green snake, turning it into a puddle of kinks and curves. I watched as it straightened itself and weaved through the grass.

I watched a lot of porn. One Saturday, with Viv out of town on some antiquing trip, I masturbated for three straight hours. I went through a time warp, lost hours, watching all the bending women and vacant men, tan, slick, violent, inside out. It was like an itchy toxin entered my brain, and everything, even the walls, seemed to be vibrating with a sex ache. I went at it with all the jumbled, smeared, neon images in my mind. I shoved myself to some end I never got to except in small, scalding increments. It was like I was trying to push a door open, a heavy wooden one with just enough bend to make me think I could do it; I shoved and slammed my shoulder against it trying to make a big enough opening to let the sun pour through, but it just wouldn't give. Fifteen tiny orgasms and one upended afternoon later I lay there with a wet back, cramped fingers, slick and depthless as a lake, displaced, deranged, and run ragged.

One night I went to an art reception at the university. I thought it wouldn't be out of the question to meet someone at an event like that. But it was really cold. There was cold white wine, and cold strawberries, and mostly only women wearing lots of colorful scarves and who knew one another, waving their arms around and wrapped up in their own concerns.

Another night I went to a hotel bar. I picked it simply because I'd driven by it a few times and it looked like the kind of place where a traveling businessman might linger for a lonely drink. It was a big chain hotel on Main Street that was trying to ingratiate itself by displaying some local color, and so called itself an old tavern, the only manifestation of which were menus printed on treasure-map-looking paper. I ordered a cocktail and sat there for half an hour by myself, reading a North Carolina travel brochure for seniors, and the only other people there were the bartender and a trio of women at a small round table next to a blue-lit aquarium. Why were there so many women everywhere?

I couldn't get the summer to work. I couldn't crank it right. There were dark, split, bloated days where I simmered with frustration. One afternoon I stared at a lady at a craft store when I was picking up some paints for Viv on the way home from work. She had jiggly arms and was wearing a stupid wooden necklace and I hated her for the pliant way she was nodding at the clerk. For being so middle-aged and obsolete and *accommodating*.

I went on another Internet date. This one was with a guy named Chance, who was a landscape architect and an altogether way more well-adjusted person than Bill had been. We met at a historic home and walked around the grounds. He pointed out stuff about the flowers and the design of the garden and seemed like a nice guy.

We took the tour, which didn't allow us to talk much. We kept stealing glances at each other and I had no idea what they meant. Afterward he told me he'd hated the tour. I, in fact, had found it really interesting. When I told him this he laughed like I was making a joke, and then looked troubled when he realized I wasn't. There were a couple more conversational misfires as we walked down the cobblestone path to the parking area. We said a quick goodbye, giving each other a light hug and getting our name tags stuck together in the process, which caused us to be in a prolonged embrace as we both frantically tried to undo them. When we finally pulled away from each other, his face was burning red. We turned and practically ran to our respective cars.

I joined the gym. I wanted to swim, to get the peace of mind that comes with exercise, but also I went in there with the unwieldy expectation that I might meet someone. It was an expensive place in town with flat-screen televisions everywhere and hard, compact employees walking around with walkie-talkies. Every bit of eye contact with a man vaguely in my age range seemed charged with possibility. But I didn't know how to pry them open, those looks, make anything out of them. There was someone—an older, lithe man, a swimmer with close-cropped gray hair—who would watch me in the lanes now and then. But when I maneuvered to pick up his towel, and then apologized, he looked at me with the kind of indifference that made me realize I'd misinterpreted the whole thing.

Every afternoon I still shoehorned myself into my business clothes and went to the office. I hardly ever saw Elliot. He used a different entrance than the others, and I did everything I could to avoid his end of the building. Once or twice he stopped by the front desk and tried to make conversation, but there was something apologetic and almost peevish about his manner now and I responded with professional, dismissive courtesy. It was too hard to deal with or acknowledge it—the sapling of possibility that had shot up in our previous interactions and that now lay inertly between us.

In desperation I signed up for a watercolor class at the university. It was on my list. It's not as if I thought it would be the kind of thing that was teeming with single, available men. But then when I thought about it I could picture some older guy, scanning the room, itchy with divorce. Plus, it was the only class that still had slots available.

My mother's voice had a self-satisfied throatiness to it I'd never heard before.

"It's *wonderful* here," she growled.

I was standing on the hot stepping-stones in the back garden, staring at a vine that had started to crawl up one side of the French doors. It was mid-July.

"Really?" I said.

"Wow, Jay," she sighed. "Yes. It is." She never called me that.

"Please don't call me that."

"It's just . . ." I felt her searching for the words. "I've never . . . Let's just say your father and I have really reconnected."

"Well, so, what's it like? What have you guys been up to?"

"What have we been up to?" She laughed. "We're like teenagers!"

I tried sitting on the stone bench, but it burned the backs of my legs, so I got up.

"When we first got here," she continued, "the place was, well, it was fine, it just wasn't what we expected." I pictured my mom making this gesture with her hand she always did, her bracelets tinkling down her wrist. "But then we met this other couple, and they told us about a different place. I said, you know, 'Doug, they're smug, they're hippies . . .' But then we said, 'Why not?' and we packed our stuff, and we moved over there. They had one little cabana sort of thing left and, long story short, we ended up going to this seminar the couple suggested, and, wow, Jay. I had no idea how much I was missing out."

"Missing out?"

"Well, I don't think I'd ever really had an orgasm before."

"I gotta go."

"Not a *real* one. Your father. He really moved me. He. Moved. Me."

"That's interesting but—"

"And it's all because we said, 'Let's get out of our comfort zone. We're here, aren't we? For something new? Well, *let's try something new.*' Our teacher, Mr. Prince, he had the most capable hands. It was in a room with a fountain in the middle. We sat on these really fun reed mats."

"Mr. Prince?"

"He was honest, and straightforward, and the whole thing was really about healing. That's what it was about."

"So this was some kind of like sex class?"

"Don't be such a prude, Jay."

"I'm not!"

"I know that you young people today have all sorts of tools and know-how, but for my generation, well, at least for my*self*—little Miss Star of Collin County—I never really knew how to let go."

"I'm glad you've figured it out."

"I'm just happy for you. I'm picturing you out there, having all sorts of affairs, getting all of this experience. I'm just happy—happy you've been able to explore your sexuality, happy that our society has *allowed* you to try different things, to try different men. Julia? Are you still there?"

"Yes."

"And that you didn't have to wait until the ripe old age of twenty-two to finally . . . Well, you probably didn't know this. I think I was always a bit embarrassed to tell you. But I was a virgin when I got married."

"Hmmm," I said. "I didn't know that."

"Can you imagine?" she said. "A virgin at twenty-two."

"Wow."

"Yep," said my mom, and she went on. They were eating cubed fruit every morning. Her skin looked amazing. I stared at the sagging trees in the distance and pictured a bunch of massive, synchronized explosions—whipping white light and people's skin melting off and vending machines collapsing like gooey plastic bubbles and windows blasting out and forests and buildings going up like tinder until everything is smoldering gristle and ash. And then, from the outside, the whole Earth, there's a laser from another universe and it all gets blown up, just fucking pulverized.

— *Nine* —

A few days later I sat with Allison Block from work in a downtown seating area with pink concrete dividers separating us from the historic main street walkway. People waded through the heat, peering into store windows. A very old man and woman walked by, hand in hand.

"Cute couple," she said, tilting her head to the side.

"Awww," I said, trying to get into the spirit.

We were people watching. It's what Allison suggested we do when I'd asked her if she wanted to get a drink. We'd always been chatty, and I thought it would be good to have a friend in town. Someone to go out with. But within five minutes of sitting down with her, I could tell she was already zipped up in her life and didn't have time for or really need another girlfriend.

"Anyway," she said. She stealthily whipped her hair around so it landed on a different shoulder and readjusted her sunglasses. "We settled on the farmhouse-style tables in the end. God. Stop me. This must be so boring for you."

"No, no! I mean, it sounds like it's like trying to organize a United Nations conference," I said. I shifted uncomfortably in my seat.

She was telling me about her wedding. She was getting married in the fall. The guy was named Caleb Clark and they met at Duke but they hadn't hit it off. It was only now, years later, when they were the only two people on some stupid ghost tour, that they'd reconnected. These were some of the things she told me. He was from a large, sprawling, storied Southern family, and his mother was addicted to sleeping pills, but it was more like a joke, just one more quirk in a cast of eccentrics because—and this is something I gathered, that she didn't tell me—they had money. Money like ancient ore in the Clark family line, money that nullified all problems and that had a home in a mansion surrounded by forty acres on an estate about thirty miles out of town. Allison had alluded to this in an under-the-breath way, but I could tell she savored it, the fact that this would be her life, that she held it in her mouth like a lemon drop. And maybe because of this, or maybe because this was just the way she *was*, her whole bearing was as peaceful as a just-made bed. And so it didn't seem right to nose in with my uncomfortable problems.

I watched an ant, trapped in the hairs on my arm. I wondered if, now that she'd fallen through all these lucky chutes, if it must have seemed preordained to her, like it would never have been any other way. I wondered if she'd ever felt like a pinball, rolling appallingly down the center of the board toward the gutter at the bottom, unable to divert into a different life.

"My aunt Viv," I offered up, "who I'm staying with, is fifty-five and she's a virgin."

"Oh, no!" said Allison, as if my hat had flown off.

That's how she would be about it. She'd be just like that, about everything, gutturally amused, like life was a tragic, funny pageant. She could afford to be that way, now that she had what she had.

I thought of Viv, on her knees, patting something down in the garden. All those years alone in that house.

"How did that happen?" she said.

"I don't know," I said, looking over her shoulder, into the distance.

"Uh-oh," she said, scrunching her face up in an amused way.

"What?"

She gestured toward something and I looked over. A man with a bunch of tattoos wearing a leather vest and a plaid skirt and holding a beat-up cardboard box was walking our way.

"Just don't make eye contact with him," I said. "He's got a bunch of plastic anime figurines in that box and he'll try to sell them to us if you seem one iota interested. So just, seriously, don't look him in the eye, it's happened to me twice."

"Okay," she said. "That shouldn't be hard."

The man passed us.

"He kind of reminds me of Elliot."

I looked at her. "From work?" I said. "Really? Why?"

"The ponytail."

"Yeah, he has a ponytail, but I would say that's the only thing they have in common."

"It's just that Elliot's is so long," she said.

"Yeah, it is pretty long."

"He thinks he's a Highland warrior or something."

"I know," I said wistfully.

"I mean, don't get me wrong, he's *nice*," she said, unscrewing the top of her sparkling water.

She was staring at me.

"What?" I said.

She smiled. "You like him."

I was playing with the side of the napkin. "No I don't!" I said. "Besides, he's married."

"Yeah," she said distantly.

She put her bottle down. "His wife, Devon, she came into the office once." She made a comically frightened expression.

"What?" I said.

"Well, first of all, she's like fifty feet tall."

"I knew it," I said. "I knew she was crazy."

"She came in holding this huge vase. I think it was supposed to be a gift? For the office? Well, they kept walking around with it. She was like, 'Put it there, no, put it there,' you know? Like kind of bossy?"

"Yeah."

"You can tell who wears the pants. The way he looked at her— just, in love, you know?"

"Yeah," I said uneasily.

We were quiet for a few moments. A large man on a small bike wobbled by.

"I'm going to set her up," I said. "My aunt."

Allison nodded, swallowing a gulp of water.

"You are?"

"Yeah."

"Do you think that's a good idea?"

"Well, why not?"

"Maybe she likes things the way they are."

"No," I said, "I don't think so."

I had to know it could happen for Aunt Viv. That the tide of bad luck, or whatever it was, could be reversed. I didn't want to do the background mental shifts to accommodate the kind of world where she'd be alone forever. If you looked at it from the outside, it made total sense—a man and a woman meeting in their late fifties and falling in love. And, on the board game of their lives, there had to be some pike or fork that diverted them into each other's path. And maybe that was supposed to be me. I had to know the pattern could be broken. The summer was more than halfway over. I felt the dark sides of my predicament pressing in on me.

An exhausted dog with its tongue hanging out walked by.

Allison tilted her head into the sun and closed her eyes. "Mmmm," she said, "it's such a nice day," as if the whole world nourished her.

—Ten—

I stared at the long nose and noble face of the watercolor teacher. She had completely white hair, swept back, and was wearing a loose-fitting flannel shirt. She looked like the kind of plain-Jane woman who still managed to elicit gritty loyalty in the men she was with. Not exactly pretty, but elegant in the way she did things. She probably had a quiet, studious way that a man would eventually fall in love with without really knowing why. She looked like she had had a lot of unself-conscious sex, like her life was racked by sex and she never even talked about it because it was such a given. I could see her being bent over things, bending, bending, bending, over a wooden horse, a sofa, laughing, her life replete, sun-soaked. She probably knew how to change a tire, and had a laugh like ribbons crumpling to the ground. I could just see her life. I could just see it.

Everyone was looking at me.

"My name is Julia," I said. "And I'm here because I wanted to try something new. I did some watercoloring once, when I was a kid, but I've forgotten how to do it since then."

"I'm Sandy," said the woman next to me. "I've had some experience, but I wanted to learn more about the technique."

"I'm Aames," said the guy next to her. "I'm here for a friend."
Everyone laughed. He had long gray hair fanned out over a tattered
jean jacket, and he looked around at everyone with a rigid, defiant
expression as if challenging us to not think he was charming.

It was the day of my first watercolor class and it had rained.
When I got to the college campus, all the redbrick pathways were
misting and people were just starting to emerge from under aw-
nings, shaking out their umbrellas. I parked and walked in what I
thought was the right direction.

The campus, sleepy during the summer, was composed of
colonial-style buildings and pleasantly unkempt trees. The building
I walked toward, however, seemed to be some kind of cubist, concrete, 1970s add-on. I passed two metal benches outside the entrance and a sculpture of suspended silver zigzags.

I took the elevator up to a big airy room on the third floor. It was
nice enough with the windows open, looking out onto all the wet,
jungly greenery outside. The smell of rain came in. Someone had
shoved a bunch of chairs and some burlap couches to one end, and
people were standing around, waiting for the teacher, some leaning against the windowsills.

Upon entering, I immediately scanned the room for possibilities. There was a mom-type with a sullen sixteen-year-old daughter.
There were a few women in business clothes chatting and eating
pasta out of Tupperware and wearing plastic badges as if they'd just
come from their jobs as health administrators; a cheerful lady, wearing linen overalls, who I just knew was going to be pleasant to talk
to; then there was the guy named Aames, with his hair fanned over
his back.

The teacher strode in wearing riding boots. Behind her was Gerald.

Gerald Campbell. There was just something so open about him. That was the first thing I noticed. He had the tentative, fragile smile of a kid who got routinely bullied and was constantly trying to make amends.

He seemed more or less my age, maybe a little older. He had a fleshy, square-shaped face. He was wearing the ill-fitting jeans of a homeschooler, or someone who had been too protected to develop a sense of cultural agility, and a thick, striped sweater. He had darting eyes and that delicate smile, and then there was a detail that would, in any other circumstance, have caused me to completely discount him—a neon-green lucky rabbit's foot hanging from his belt loop.

None of this would usually have added up to anything resembling the type of guy I would have wanted to be in any type of heavy-breathing situation with, but ever since the conversation with my mom I'd felt a dark, locked-down sense of purpose. I watched him lean his watercolor pad against the wall, look hopefully around, and apologize to no one in particular when his keys fell to the floor. It was the time for action, and here was a nice, eager, sweet-looking guy. Not exactly the man of my dreams, but someone who would work for a once-off, an anonymous encounter.

I was further emboldened when he introduced himself. "I'm Gerald," he said. "I just moved to town, and I thought I'd just get out there and try something new." His voice was really low and a little gravelly, which dispelled his slightly uncooked exterior a little.

I attempted to set my easel—an unwieldy wooden thing I'd had to lug from a corner of the room—next to his, in a way that I hoped didn't seem too obvious, although I had a feeling that the sixteen-year-old girl, who was shooting looks my way, knew exactly what I was doing the whole time.

We all hauled out paints and palettes and brushes from a supply closet and set everything up. Our teacher began the class with a demonstration in which she created flower petals with simple dabs of the brush.

"I like your rabbit's foot," I said to him, once we got started. In the tumult of getting ready, the class had proven to be a jovial one, with everyone sort of cheerily apologizing for getting in each other's way, and talking and complimenting one another on their progress. There was enough chatter going on, with the teacher walking slowly around the circle to offer tips, that starting a conversation with the person next to me did not seem to ripple anything in a strange way.

"Ah, thank you, thank you," he said, looking down at it. "My brother gave it to me. He said it was good luck, and so I started wearing it, and now I'm afraid to take it off."

"I understand," I said, which was true. This was just the kind of superstitious nonsense I could relate to.

Next he offered something: "Have you seen her work?" he said, indicating our teacher. I could tell he didn't think we were flirting yet.

"No," I said. "You mean, is she like locally famous or something?"

"I looked her up. She won the North Carolina stamp design competition."

"No kidding." I watched the teacher; she was leaning over the girl, pointing at something on her canvas. "I didn't know any old person off the street could design a stamp."

"Well, what with budget cuts and everything," he said. His eyes cut to me.

I laughed. "What would you design? If you had to make a stamp."

"Hmmm." He seemed to take the question very seriously. "Maybe a bird, the state bird. What about you?"

"For North Carolina? Maybe like an old . . . barn."

He smiled. "I like it."

"You're really off-roading there," I said about ten minutes later, pointing at his pad, on which he'd painted a lizard walking up the side of the page, with squiggles around it to indicate its zany passage.

He burst out laughing. And then I saw him look at me in a new way, size me up as a possibility, and then immediately extinguish any thought that I might be coming on to him.

I liked the warmth in his eyes. He had such a completely different feeling about him than Bill Meeks did. Bill was filled with compacted, frantic resentment, and this person was all trust and light and belief and the sense that anything was worth a try.

"I want to design logos," he said.

"Really?"

He nodded.

"That's nice," I said. "That's nice and specific. Do you have anything in mind? Any logos you've got in the pipeline?"

"Well." He got kind of serious. "I've been thinking about it. I have one idea—it would be for contact lenses?"

I nodded.

"Just for any brand. You always see people putting them in, in the commercials. And clear green fields and things like that. But I was thinking, there could be a little blue guy."

"A little blue guy?" I said.

"Yeah," he said. "As the logo." He nodded to himself. "And he would be on the box and everything."

"Sure, yeah," I said. "What would he be doing?"

"What do you mean?"

"I mean, on the box."

"I don't know," said Gerald. "Maybe, sitting on a porch swing? Or, standing next to a windmill."

I waited for him to go on.

"Cool," I said. "Maybe he could be leaning against the letters, causing them to jumble together."

Gerald considered it. It dawned on him. "Yeah," he said. "I like that."

"Or lying on top of them. Like he's just *been* lying on top of them."

He nodded. "That's good, too. Anyway," he said. "It's just one idea I have. I have to think about it more."

"I think it's really good," I said. "You've got to start somewhere."

"Yeah." He laughed a little. "I guess so."

There was something else about the way he looked at me—a slight, decorous pulling back, as if he didn't want me to think he expected anything out of our flirting. I could feel it. If it was going to be him, I was going to have to be the one to make a move.

I thought about it for the last half hour of the class. I was getting nervous. I kept looking at the clock above the chalkboard. Soon people would start gathering their things. I didn't want to wait another week for something to happen—here was a man, we were flirting, and this was exactly what I had come here this summer to do. Of all the possible ways it could happen, of all the different men and varieties of the experience, a nice guy in a thick sweater from an art class was not the worst of all possible outcomes.

I was getting so focused on the end of the class that I was clamming up, going rigid while trying to bend myself into affecting the right kind of measured nonchalance.

Luckily, he gave me an in, and I went ahead and took the plunge.

"Crap," he said, looking down at his rabbit's foot, which was splattered with a little paint.

"It'll come out," I said.

"This was my favorite one." He looked up at me while unclipping it from his belt and wrapping it in some newspaper. "I have a collection."

"Of rabbit's feet?"

"Yup."

"I'd like to see it sometime."

For a moment he seemed terrified. And then it dawned on him, what was happening. "You should."

Strangely, I felt proud of him.

"When?" I said.

And then it happened so quickly, the way we made plans and exchanged numbers, as if we were both trying to trap something.

We looked at each other, both a little embarrassed, smiling.

I had it all planned out.

Viv and I sat across from each other, a few days after the water-color class, at a restaurant that had fashioned itself like a French bistro. Smudged mirrors with lightbulbs around them hung on the walls, shedding a golden, cheerful glow. It was rainy outside and the windows were fogged up and it was humid. Viv's hair was frizz-ier than usual, but she looked nice. She was wearing a silk blouse with a faint zebra print, and a necklace made of green stones and dangling, antique-looking earrings. They were swinging back and forth. She put up her hands to still them. "I think it should be incor-porated more into our general vocabulary," she said, "'My personal Hillary Step,' that kind of thing."

She was telling me about a book on Mount Everest she was read-ing, and the people who have climbed it. We were on our first glass of wine, and color was leaping into her face.

"Yeah, that would be useful," I said. "You could say, 'Getting past that performance exam was a real Hillary Step.'"

"Exactly," she said.

"It sounds good," I said.

"I got it from Melayna," she said.

"Who?" I said, kidding.

"Melayna," she said.

"Yeah, no, I know."

"She's turned out to be interesting," said Viv, with authority. She sat back and looked around in a pleased, dignified manner. "I like it here," she said. "How did you find it? I never hear of these things."

"There was an article about it in the paper," I said. "The weekly one."

A woman with a wet umbrella and hair plastered to her head walked by, brushing our table with her wet raincoat.

I shook my leg up and down under the table. I looked at my watch. In about twenty minutes, if things went according to plan, Gordon was going to show up with my sunglasses. I'd planted them at his store that morning, made a point of going there before work. Then that afternoon, I'd called the store and told him I'd left them there, and would he mind just bringing them by the restaurant right around the corner where Viv and I were going to be eating dinner?

I figured, maybe Viv just needed someone to shove her out of this cycle of misunderstanding she had with Gordon, someone to kick the whole thing into gear and get it ticking the right way. She'd seemed touched when I asked her out to dinner, my treat, to thank her for letting me stay there over the summer. Once we were all sitting together, and they'd started with their rapport, I would put down a bunch of cash, make up some excuse, and leave. All they needed was to be sitting across from each other, with a few glasses of wine between them. I needed to know this could happen.

"Except"—Viv sat forward again—"she has this sand garden. That she keeps at the front desk. I swear, it's driving me up the wall." We were still talking about Melayna. "She scrapes it back and forth, back and forth, and I can hear it from across the hall. Sometimes I want to go over there and take it and chuck it into the trash and just see what she does."

I had a flash of what Viv would have been like in college, when

she was young: daring and no-nonsense, probably really into theater, easily hurt, noble. A great friend.

"That would drive me crazy, too," I said.

A waiter came and took down our orders for appetizers. A ceiling fan turned listlessly above. I played with my napkin and checked
the time on my phone. Gordon should have closed up already, if he
kept to the hours on his website. Maybe a customer was keeping
him late. Next to us, a waiter cleaned a wineglass with his apron.

I could tell Viv thought I seemed distracted, but I couldn't help
turning around to look at the front of the restaurant, toward the
door. As soon as I turned back to her she said, "Oh, God, it's
Gordon," and her face flashed with something that looked an
awful lot like irritation. I looked behind me again; he was weaving
through the tables.

"Yes it is!" I said, facing her again. I tried to smile. "Actually, I told
him to come here."

She raised her eyebrows at me, confused.

"I left my sunglasses at his store this morning," I said, too cheerfully, "and I told him to bring them by. I thought he could join us
and . . ." I trailed off.

By the time he arrived at our table, cleanly shaven, wearing a
button-down shirt sprinkled with rain, it had dawned on her what
was going on and she looked cornered, stricken.

"Gordon," she said blankly.

"Hi!" I said. "Join us."

He moved into a chair next to Viv.

Viv was completely still and barely acknowledged him when
he sat down. She seemed to be focusing on her hand, which sat like

an inanimate object on the table. We all stared at it for a moment. There was something parasitic and almost goblin-like about Gordon now, like he'd affixed himself to the side of our night.

"Thank you, thank you so much," I said loudly. "For bringing me my sunglasses."

"Of course," said Gordon, producing them from a plastic bag.

I wanted to rewind, erase, go back. To save Viv from having to do anything, I started talking quickly about some of the things I'd seen in Gordon's store, trying to engage him so she could get her bearings. At the very least, she could just endure through dinner and then I could apologize or maybe we wouldn't have to talk about it and the whole thing could just get swallowed by the summer.

"I've never seen such cool vintage sports posters," I said. "They used to really do things differently, you know? What's that one? That you have in the window?"

"French Open, 1923," said Gordon. "That's a designer named Lee Steeple. Dead now, of course. Those are pretty hard to get."

Someone in the corner of the restaurant popped a bottle of champagne.

By now Gordon had sensed something was wrong, and we were both animatedly ignoring silent Viv, pretending to have a buoyant conversation and stealing looks at her. Our waiter came and dropped off our appetizers. Gordon didn't order anything.

"He had a terrible drinking problem," Gordon said. "He designed a poster, at the end of his life, his most famous one—for the Spassky-Fischer tournament of 1972. With the chess pieces made to look like mountains? Maybe you've seen it?"

I shook my head.

"But, no, it was the drinking," said Gordon.

"Right, right."

"The First World War. He saw too much, they say." I felt terrible for Gordon, for the position I'd put him in. It was like watching someone on a unicycle—him trying to get through this conversation.

"Jeez, yeah," I said. "What a war. What a war."

Viv's eyes flashed to me with a complicated mix of amusement and resentment. She was starting to listen to us.

"I mean, I don't even know why that war happened," I said. "I think I remember learning about it, but nothing stuck. It's like Austria-Hungary, Prussia, *what*? It's like a bar of soap that slips out of my hand, when I think about it." I took a gulp of my wine. "Not that I think about the start of World War One in the shower that much, ha-ha." I felt myself go red.

"Balance of powers," said Viv. We both looked at her. She was haughtily playing with the edge of her cloth napkin.

Gordon saw his opening. "Is that so?" He leaned in a little. "I always thought it was the rivalry between England and Germany."

"That's what I mean," she said. Then, directly to Gordon, "That's one thread. But now they're saying there's no one culprit. It was more like a broth, of patriotism, fear, swashbuckling empires, everyone thought through their own moral arithmetic they were in the right."

Viv kept talking, and by the time she got to Archduke Ferdinand, she was starting to get into her element. She was talking in the kind of bossy but charming way she used with her friends, basking in our attention, benevolently parceling out eye contact. Gordon was listening, wrapped up in it. "And the more you look into it, the more you ask 'how' not 'why,' and the more specifics you get, the more you realize you're back where you started, that there is no overriding logic," she said. He peppered her with questions. The waiter came and went. We had dinner. Gordon ordered a glass of wine. Little by little, Viv unwound.

"I wish I could have been there, on the eve of that war," he said at one point. "To know what the air was like."

"Me too," said Viv. "To get that sense of the gears turning, what was *really* happening."

"It reminds me of that line from *Macbeth*," said Gordon.

"That's my favorite one!" she said. "Which line?" She touched her ear again. Some hair was coming out from where it was tied back. She looked at Gordon generously. I could see her taking stock, pleased, warming to the idea of the night. Maybe I was right. Maybe this was all they needed. I could picture myself leaving in a little while, letting them take it from here.

"'I am so far stepped in blood,'" he quoted.

"No, no," interrupted Viv, laughing. "It's 'I am in blood stepped in so far.'"

"No it's not," he said, also laughing. "I am so far stepped in blood, that—"

"You're wrong." She vigorously shook her head. "It is, and I quote . . ." Her cheeks were red and her whole being was billowing, proud as a flag. She said, in a loud, oratorical voice: "'I am in blood stepped in so far, that should I wade no more, returning were as tedious as go o'er.'" At the last word, she did a flourish with her hand and knocked over a glass of wine.

Seeing the effect all of this had on Gordon—how he retreated, almost imperceptibly—was like watching a sports play in slow motion, a football grazing someone's fingertips, the awed pain of a near miss. Her red hair fizzed down her shoulders, her face flared. She was like a storm. And the way she'd fixed on this thing, it was too much for him, too intense. He scratched the back of his head. "Yeah, you're probably right," he said. He looked around evasively. He yawned and leaned back.

Viv held for a moment, her eyes sparkling, waiting for him to give her the right reaction. But he had left her out there on the field, alone.

Confused, disoriented, she drew back, and looked around quickly.

I wanted to slap him, to shake him, to throw water in his face. Why couldn't he just meet her there, at that register, either because he was having as much fun or just to be nice?

It seemed that the restaurant had become completely quiet. Viv started quickly dabbing at the circle of red wine on the tablecloth. I did, too, trying to help.

"O'er?" I said, trying to smile brightly. "What does that mean? Is that a word? Is that a Shakespeare word?"

"Over there," she said, not looking up. "Or in this context, over."

We continued. The night continued. We all tried to make conversation. To the outside eye, nothing appeared to be different. Gordon, I think he felt bad, straightened himself out and tried to talk to Viv more, but his motions now had the feel of a forced courtliness. Eventually, in the corner of the restaurant, a band started playing, and we watched them, not really talking, each of us uneasy in our own way. Had it all really deflated? Or was I just imagining it? It contributed to the feeling I'd been having all summer: a lack of proportion, a loss of a sense of scale. I couldn't tell anymore what was a big deal and what didn't mean anything.

We left Gordon at the front of the restaurant and drove home together. Viv had been perfectly pleasant to him when we said goodbye, but now she was quiet. The rain had stopped but the sky was dark with cloud cover. She stared out at the side of the road. We drove in silence. I opened the window and let in the thick, knitted air of late summer. I wanted to apologize, but I felt that it would acknowledge everything I had done, everything that had happened—how she hadn't even wanted to be drawn in but had gamely stepped up to the plate, only to be rejected by someone she wasn't even interested in. I didn't want to admit that I had been the cause of any of that, and maybe the narrative to stick to was just that it was a pleasant, if sometimes strained, night with an acquaintance. So I glanced over at her and didn't say anything. When we got home, she said, "Thank you, that was very nice," in a tight way, and went up to bed. Soon after, I went up, too.

The next day I stood in a small art gallery attached to a sandwich shop, waiting for them to call my name with my order, and stared at an acrylic painting of a bowl of fruit. One of the pieces of fruit had a face and was wearing a court jester's hat.

"Chance Moon Lively," said someone behind me.

I turned around. It was Elliot.

"You're always doing that," I said.

"Doing what?"

"Coming up behind me and saying something."

"Oh," he said. "Well, it's the name of the artist."

"Well, it's the worst thing I've ever seen," I said, and moved to the next painting, another acrylic of a mythic, godlike man holding a lightning bolt, sitting hunched over at a bar.

Elliot was holding a salad in a plastic tub, and here, out of the office and in the light of day, he looked hunched and smaller. His ponytail was pulled especially tight, and I thought I saw some flakes of dry skin where his hair parted.

"He's a good friend of mine," he said.

"Oh," I said.

"Just kidding." He smiled.

I didn't want to take the baton and fall into some kind of warm banter with him. I walked to the next painting.

"What, are you really plugged into the local art scene or something?" I said.

"Sort of," he said, following me. "I actually do know a few people who do stuff. I have a couple friends who own galleries." He pointed at the lightning bolt painting. "This can be yours for only five hundred dollars."

"What a steal," I said.

A woman with a greasy braid and a pinched expression came up to us. She looked at a receipt. "Julia Greenfield?" she said.

"Yes?"

"Your sandwich is ready. We've been calling your name for ten minutes," she said.

"Oh, sorry," I said. "I've just been in here."

"Well, this isn't technically part of the shop."

"Oh, okay," I said.

She turned and walked away. Elliot was smiling at me. I could tell he wanted for us to be in this moment together, for it to be something we could laugh about, build on. There was something I found unpleasant about his manner—holding a salad, unevenly trying to hit on me when he had a wife.

"Well," I said, "I better go get my sandwich."

"Hey," he said, more seriously, blocking my way. "I've been meaning— I wanted to say thanks, again, for the gift you gave me. The sand thingy."

"Sandscape," I said.

"What was that?"

"It's called a sandscape. I finally figured out what they're called."

"Right," he said. "And you can move it—I mean, if you turn it over, it just creates a different picture."

"Well, that's your prerogative," I said.

"Hey," he said. He motioned with his salad. "After you get your sandwich, do you want to walk to the park together?"

His bearing, the way he asked me, was somehow acknowledging everything that had gone on between us—my crush on him and how I hadn't caught on that he was married, and I got the sense that he felt sorry for me and was just trying to make me feel better. To be friends. All of this made me angry and I wanted to leave.

"I can't," I said, turning back to him. "I have to meet someone."

"Oh, okay," he said, disappointed. He hesitated. "I wanted— I've been meaning to tell you . . ." I tilted my head. But then something shifted inside him and he retreated. "Never mind."

The door to the gallery creaked open and a couple of people walked in. We both watched them for a second.

"Well," I said, "I'll see you later."

"Okay, sure," he said. And I left him standing there.

It turned out that my date with Gerald was on the hottest day of the year, during an already record-breaking summer. I stared out the window of my bedroom, combing my hair, and thought about how much I didn't want to go outside and get into my baking car. Everything about this idea now seemed deflated and futile.

We'd decided to meet at a coffee shop and then go from there to his house. I swayed down Main Street at approximately two o'clock in the breezeless afternoon. The storefronts were unpleasantly bright and everything felt smeared. I saw someone listlessly walking their dog, but otherwise it was deserted. My shirt stuck to my back. I felt a little sick. The heat made the empty street feel like another planet, hostile to life.

When I got to the coffee shop and opened the door and recovered from the blast of air-conditioning, I saw him sitting at a table, staring out the window with that same smile.

On my way out there, I'd tried to remember how it was in the class—how we were actually flirting, how I actually started liking him without having to contort myself too much. I remembered his low voice and unaffected manner. I was hoping we would build on our time in there. That our flirtation would layer and gain momentum and we would tap into whatever we had that afternoon. That we would actually get along and the promise of that unexpected spark would be fulfilled. I was hoping.

But the minute I walked inside and the door slammed behind me and he kind of tentatively stood up from his table, my heart fell a little. There was something pleading in his eyes. I sensed that same fragility in him from before. I immediately wanted to leave.

"Hi!" I said. "I'm just going to . . ." and I motioned toward the coffee counter.

"Sure, sure," he said.

I ordered an expensive iced drink even though now I was freezing, the sweat on my back having turned cold from the AC.

I sat down across from him. The shop was made out of fresh beams of pale wood and glass. There were serene squares of light on the floor. Aside from the employees, we were the only people there. Gerald nodded a little and smiled and leaned back. He had opaque wraparound sunglasses pushed back on his head, and they revealed two inlets of shiny forehead where his otherwise thick hair was retreating. We were both quiet for a few seconds. There was a clatter outside as an old-fashioned car with a bunch of cans attached to it drove by.

"It's hot," I said.

Gerald looked bewildered for a moment and then exploded into agreement. "Yeah! I know. It really is."

"Are you from there?" I pointed to a key chain on the table. It was a little rubber oval that read "Sonoma."

"Yeah, yeah, I am," he said. "I just moved here about a month ago. But yeah, I grew up there."

"What's it like?"

"Ah," he laughed. "It's nice. It's a good place to grow up. Do you play?"

"Play?"

He gestured at the table, which had an inlaid checkers board on the surface.

"No. Yeah," I said. "I mean, I know how to move the pieces around."

"Great!" He produced, from below the table, a velvet pouch and started withdrawing chips. I was grateful for the time this bought, how it allowed us to concentrate on something else.

"Looks like we're missing one," he said.

"We could improvise, use a coin or saltshaker or something."

He erupted into laughter again and looked at me with bald admiration. "You're terrific," he said.

We ended up using a packet of sugar and started playing while also trying to make conversation. The motor finally caught and we got to talking. This is what I learned: Gerald told me, in a stilted way, wherein I had to fill in some of the gaps, that he was raised in a very strict Mormon household out in Sonoma, California, where all his friends and everyone in his community was Mormon. It was very sheltered and close-knit and many things were not allowed and at a point in the recent past, fueled by doubts about his religion, he decided he wanted to see the rest of the world. This caused a major rupture in his family, who said they wouldn't talk to him if he left the church. He did anyway, and from what I gathered had been a bit rudderless ever since, taking an IT job here and there, and acting on half-thought-out plans.

I was pretty gripped by this story, which he told with some reluctance and shyness, turning a penny over and over in his hands. I thought it showed a depth and restlessness in him—to break away from your family like that, to have the courage to act on the itch of doubt that must have plagued him for so long. But sadness, too, to have left everything he knew and held close.

"Wow," I said, after he finished talking, my mind racing, trying to think of something to say. "I cannot relate. To. Any. Of. That."

"You were raised without religion?"

"My family was Catholic," I said. "I was baptized and confirmed. But then my parents just gradually stopped practicing, and I never really missed it that much. My mom still goes to church sometimes. I miss the music, actually. I do miss that."

"Uh-huh," he said, nodding, looking down. I felt like I should have been able to parlay his story into something else, some larger conversation about religion, something to push us over the brink of actually connecting to each other on which we were now teetering.

The door opened and closed. I looked behind me. A woman holding a giant vintage clock walked in.

When conversation is easy, it's easy. When it's hard, it's hard. But what about when it's just in-between? Flaring from the bellows of shared experience, but just as quickly stalling out?

I continued trying to find a comfortable position in my small chair, shoving it forward and back, crossing and recrossing my legs.

We finally came to a natural stopping point. As we got up from that table, he kept his eyes on me, smiling that trembling smile, as if looking for guidance.

We walked outside and started wading through the heat.

"Which way?" I asked.

He shoved his hand into his pocket and withdrew his keys.

"My car's just around the corner," he said.

"Your car?"

"Yeah."

"I thought you lived down the street."

"I do," he said. "It's just bit of a walk in this weather."

I hesitated but decided, at the time, that it made sense.

We reached his car and got inside and it was spotless. "Is this a rental?" I asked. He shook his head. "Nope."

We pulled into the street and he started driving down Main and we were both strangely silent, as if we knew what was going to happen and were forgoing any formalities. It occurred to me then that neither of us had said anything again about the lucky rabbit's foot collection, that I just got into a car with a complete stranger, and that no one knew where I was. I hadn't even left a note for Aunt Viv.

I kept expecting him to pull over, or turn off somewhere. The sun illuminated some dusty handprints on his dashboard I hadn't seen before. I was feeling more and more uneasy. "Where do you live?" I finally asked.

"It's coming right up. Just a few more miles."

Obviously, in his sheltered upbringing, Gerald had not developed a sensitivity to the flares that might go up in a woman's mind, should she witness certain behaviors in a man driving her out of town—like flexing his jaw and gripping the steering wheel and staring straight ahead without saying anything.

It also occurred to me how the other side of fragility can be tremendous violence in a person, and I pictured him bashing my head in with a snow globe in a fit of rage.

Calm down, I told myself. It's not *likely* that Gerald is a psychopath.

We finally turned into a complex, one of the new housing developments that were popping up on the outskirts of the city. It was a series of rows of town houses, with about a square foot of yard in front of each of them. At the entrance we passed a freshly painted sign that read "Madison's Ridge" in elegant, slanted writing. There were still little orange construction flags here and there, and mounds of red dirt that hadn't healed into landscaping grass. It felt eerily empty. A plastic sheet blew by.

Gerald must have read my mind. "It's a new neighborhood," he said. "I'm one of the first to move in."

"Does it have a lot of amenities?" I said.

"Ha! Yeah."

We parked in front of one of the houses and got out. He opened and shut his mailbox without really looking in, and we walked up the walkway. Inside, the apartment had a serene feel, with light falling on the carpet from large windows. It was pretty empty. There wasn't anything on the walls. It didn't look like anyone had moved in, but rather just stashed some furniture in the room. There was a flat-screen television and a black leather couch and a flimsy-looking side table. A disproportionate amount of cords ran across the floor.

About five minutes later we were drinking lemonade on his back deck. He'd poured us both a glass from the only thing in his fridge—a carton of juice.

We could see the other back decks of the other town houses, all in a row. The whole development was situated on a swell of land, not quite a hill. No one else was outside. It was thunderingly quiet. I felt like we were in the middle of nowhere, the last two people on earth, that we hadn't gotten the memo about something.

Gerald was standing next to a newly bought grill as if he meant for me to notice it. I put my lemonade down on a glass table and looked at him. It was now or never. We both felt it.

"So where's the collection?" I asked.

"Oh, yeah, that," he said in an oily way. He put his drink down, and then came over to me, and in an embarrassing, theatrical way, pushed me against the sliding glass door and started kissing me. I finally had, in that moment, insight into his whole orientation toward this thing—the collection *was* just an excuse for me to come over. This whole day *was* based on the supposition that we were going to hook up, have sex, whatever. And by the bumbling draft of passion with which he kissed me, I could tell that he thought this whole time we'd both been simmering with desire. Why else would I have been so bold in the watercolor class? Why else would I have gotten into his car? And he was now, finally, breaking the seal, expecting it to all flow out.

We knocked over a terra-cotta pot that spilled out a mound of black dirt.

I was doing the bare minimum to keep apace, which was actually quite a lot, considering all the effort he was putting into it.

It was all wrong, but I was still in a state of shock, just trying to deal with the situation at hand. The sun kept flooding into my eyes. I felt like I was trying to get my bearings underwater.

He pulled away and looked at me with such raw passion that I was mortified. He took my hand, coyly swiveled around, placed my arm on his shoulder, and said, "Follow me." As he led me into the house, I tripped on the doorway and knew something with complete certainty, something that had been hovering around my mind that I hadn't let myself fully consider—that Gerald, too, was a virgin.

Get out of here, Julia. Just leave, I said to myself, as we walked up the dark, carpeted stairs. But I was somehow unable to change the flow of the current. And another, distant, calculating part of me thought, You're so close. You're so close now. This could be it. This was going to be it.

His room was just as bare as it was downstairs. A window looked out onto the bright roof. There was a large poster of Dalai Lama quotes in different fonts.

His bed was covered with a baby blue comforter. There was the smell of air freshener. It was too cold. Gerald sat on the edge of the bed and started daintily untying his shoelaces, leaving me stranded there.

He looked up, his eyes wet with admiration, and held out his hand. I moved toward him, a bit wobbly, as if walking a plank.

We eased down onto our backs. He leaned over and shoved his hand up my shirt and held my breast and started kneading it. I mechanically lifted an arm and touched the side of his head. Even that felt too intimate, the surface of his hair, like I was touching someone's son.

I thought, There is someone out there for you, Gerald. Someone kind and wonderful who can get in step with your strange tempo of swagger and fragility, and that person is not me.

He traced the top of my underwear. To keep going, I had to keep so much at the front of my mind, had to keep so many plates suspended and spinning in the air. He eased my shirt off, and now my bare back was on the cold comforter. He reached around me to undo my bra. He was having trouble, and so he yanked at it, harder and harder. He had a rigid half smile on his face and his eyes were closed but now they opened and as I twisted my arm back to help him our heads bumped and he looked at me with utter help-lessness. I tried to smile and finally got my bra undone. I wrestled myself down on that bed, to stay, to not spring up. He was at my side, holding one of my breasts; he pulled away and, having re-gained some composure, he traced a small scar on my shoulder and then he giggled. "Uh-oh," he said, in a singsong way, and looked at me like I was a toddler. The air-conditioning clicked on, a low hum swept across the room. I focused on the bare wall. "What did you do?" he said, and I got a glimpse into the way he wanted this to go, the way he'd always thought it was going to go: fatherly sparring, I was to be a fragile, adorable thing. My eyes darted around frantically.

I sat bolt upright.

"I have to go," I said. "I'm sorry."

"Okay, okay," he said quickly, guiltily, backing away like I was a live grenade. He was looking at me in that way again. Expecting something more, helpless.

"I have, um"—I swiveled a foot into a shoe—"this thing I have to go to, with my aunt? I just completely forgot about it."

"Okay," he said, clapping his hands together, nodding.

"It's . . . She has a class? At the McGregor Art Center? And I have to bring her a cactus. So they can use it in a still life?"

"Okay," said Gerald. He put up his hands. "Okay."

A few minutes later, as he followed me down the stairs, as if by some instinct to adhere this experience to what it was originally supposed to be, to save us from some embarrassment, maybe just to prove that there was one all along, he asked if I wanted to see the collection.

"Oh, yeah, sure," I said.

He took me into the kitchen and opened a drawer. And there they were. All strewn around. A few were on chains, a few weren't. One was hot pink. One had a zebra pattern. They were matted and straggly, about ten furry rabbit's feet. I don't think I'd ever felt so lonely, in my whole life, as I did right then.

We drove back to the coffee shop in silence. He put on the radio and left it on a station that was playing festive steel drum music. When we were there, I got out and we said businesslike goodbyes. Neither of us pretended we would see each other at the watercolor class again.

On my way home in my own car, as I drove farther out of town and everything got undulating and green, I decided—I was just going to ask her. That's all there was to it. I was going to ask Aunt

Viv why she was still a virgin and then it would no longer be a mystery to me, along with the origins of the universe, buried under the dunes of her face, swallowed to the very core of her.

I was going to find her and ask her and I didn't care if it was rude or none of my business or if it would tear something between us. I was going to exhume the inexhumable. I was going to shout it at her. Because I needed to know how the impossible became possible because the horrible truth is that I thought I did know—a series of stall-outs, of things not being quite right, an endless line of Gerald Campbells.

I wanted to find her and ask her because the whole time I'd thought there had to be a reason, and the thing I was realizing with dreadful clarity, the worst of all possible outcomes, was that there simply didn't have to be a reason.

I pulled into the driveway and got out and slammed the car door shut. I was prepared to look all over for her and I stomped up the porch stairs because I didn't want to lose my resolve. I opened the door and threw my bag to the side. It was quiet and cool in the house and there she was. To my left. In the lounge. She was sitting on the couch, her hand paused midair and holding a picture and she'd been crying. A lot. Her face was shucked and raw and red. Her mouth looked like something sawed off.

"Vivienne," I said. "What is it?"

"It's Alice," she said. "She died."

After she told me about Alice, I hovered there, not knowing what to say. She seemed, for a moment, her face in complete disarray, to look to me as if I were holding the key to everything and just wasn't giving it to her.

"Is there anything I can do?" I said. But then she turned her head to the side, and by subtle grades composed herself. It was as if I'd caught her in an angle of grief that surprised us both.

She walked slowly upstairs to her bedroom and didn't come out for the rest of the day. For the next seventy-two hours it seemed as if the whole house was suffused with fragility and grief. I tried to be very quiet, and to leave her alone.

Over the next few days, with a kind of grim resolve, she threw herself into a number of household tasks: re-grouting the tiles in her bathroom, scrubbing the inside of all the kitchen drawers, stripping and painting the porch swing an adobe orange that didn't go with anything else. I'd come downstairs and find her on her knees in the kitchen, on some plastic sheeting, wiping her forehead with her shirtsleeve, and everything about her manner said she didn't want to be interrupted, go away.

"Your father and I are getting separated."

"What?" I was on the phone with my mom, in the dim living room, staring out the window at Viv, who was in her sun hat, trying to dig something out of the earth with a spade.

I put a glass of water to my cheek. "What happened? What about all that stuff you said before?"

"That was bullshit. I don't know what got into me. We're not those kind of people."

I shifted my weight, the floor creaked beneath. "I don't get it."

"Look, another couple approached us, they asked if we wanted to participate in some kind of orgy. Your father wanted to. I did not. Let's just say it exposed some fault lines."

"Dad said that?"

"I wanted to tell you first. I know it's not what you want to hear, but the truth is we've been having trouble for a while." She sounded out of breath. I pictured her throwing stuff into a duffel bag in a frenzy. "Your father is an idiot. No, I take that back. I'm sorry I said that. But, hold on." She muffled the phone. "It's on the hammock," I heard her yell. "That hammock! Hold on, Julia. The *hammock*," she screamed.

"I'm back. But, Julia, what I wanted to say is that we'll both be there for you, okay? This isn't going to affect anything between us and you."

"But I mean. I just— Wait."

I sat down. I bunched up my skirt in my hand, then let it go.

"What's going to happen?" I said. "Is one of you going to move?"

"Your father is going to spend some time with the Cargills."

"He's going to Miami?"

"It's what we could arrange at the last minute."

I pictured my dad standing at an outdoor bar, wearing a lime-green blazer and glancing around hopefully. I felt terribly, terribly sad.

"Are you there?"

"It's just— I'm really surprised. I'm shocked," I said.

I got up and looked out the window again. Viv was digging up a flower bed. I watched her yank a plant out of the ground, inspect its leaves, and toss it to the side. I turned and ran my finger along the lacquered top of a cabinet, making a line through the dust.

My mom sighed. "It's hard to explain." There was a raggedy, tired edge to her voice now.

"Yeah," I said.

"When you first get married, you have all these expectations. When I first met your father—and this isn't his fault, it's my fault." She seemed unsure of how to go on. "I don't think I've ever told you this, but the first time I saw him was at a party at the Sedleckies'. Remember them? It was in their living room. They had this great fire going, and I'd never been to a place like that. Doug was standing there, with a drink, wearing his glasses. He looked so at home in that environment. He looked at me, and then maybe it was the alcohol, but he suggested everyone go outside and play horseshoes. And I thought—I'm not sure if this will make any sense—that that's how it was always going to *be.*"

"I'm not sure I understand."

"You make these implicit promises," she said. "You don't say them out loud."

"But it's been thirty years, Mom."

"I know," she said. "And it hasn't necessarily been a bad thirty years."

We were quiet for a few moments. I thought of our house in Texas. It had pink carpeting and there was a saddle on the wall and it was decorated with cow skulls and other Western things and had a sparse, warm feeling and I wondered about this unraveling between my parents. I wondered when it had started happening.

"Remember that trip we took, when you were little, to the Smoky Mountains?"

"Not really."

"You must have been six or seven. You could see them in the distance, as we were driving there. We pointed them out to you and said, 'That's where we're going,' and you got this look on your face—you were so excited."

"Okay."

"When we finally got there, you kept looking around like you were confused. You kept asking, 'Are we in the mountains?' and we said, 'Yes, honey, we're here.'"

"What are you saying?" I said, but I knew what she was talking about. I remembered—the misty blue layers in the distance, as we were driving. It was like something from a historical movie. Something that would go with sweeping music. But when we got there the ground felt as flat as it had been before. There were more trees, but the land around us, that I could see, felt more or less the same.

"Things are different sometimes, when you get there, than you expect them to be."

I sat back down and smoothed my skirt. I looked at my feet. I looked at the ridges on my fingernails.

"How do you think he thought it was going to be with you?" I said.

"With me?" She seemed taken aback. She sighed. I stared at the light hitting a Chinese vase on a side table. "I think he thought I was going to be nurturing," she said. "And the friends I had at the time—I tricked him, too—I think he thought I was going to be the life of the party."

— *Eleven* —

It was the first day of August and the afternoon of Alice's funeral and reception, and the sky was a harsh, undifferentiated white. People stood around in clumps on the sloping front lawn, squinting and drinking lemonade from plastic cups and pulling at their shirts.

The service had been held at a stuffy Unitarian church in the middle of town, with a minister droning, and the sound of hammering wafting in from construction taking place across the street. A picture of Alice, blown up and on a pedestal, showed her in her younger days at a youth camp, standing in a muddy corral, her arms around a bunch of teenagers wearing bright-neon-green T-shirts, a horse in the background.

I wasn't quite sure what to say to Aunt Viv that morning as we got into the car. She appeared to be holding it together pretty well, except for now and then she would seem, her eyes welling, momentarily helpless. "Here," I said, as we sat down, and I took an old coffee cup out of the holder between the seats. I'd left it there when I borrowed Viv's car the other day. I dashed inside to throw it away. I felt like I needed to give her a minute and some sort of act of attention and small generosity to show what I couldn't say, and when I got back, she had her hands on the steering wheel and was staring grimly ahead.

She was wearing a black dress with a too-small embroidered vest of the kind a mariachi singer might wear. It was boxy at the shoulders and the sleeves came to just below her elbows. I wanted to go back to earlier that morning and interfere with whatever reasoning had caused her to fish it out of whatever plastic storage bag it had been in. Especially because she was obviously too hot—little slicks of sweat appeared in the creases of her neck.

We were both sluggish from the torpor of the funeral when we pulled up to Karen's house. I looked out at all the people on the front lawn and the endless afternoon unrolled before me. I needed to find somewhere quiet where I could be by myself. Some kind of cool, dark study or attic room.

The house was large and old with a pretty, rambling garden. Two muscular dogs charged up the lawn and into the entrance, upsetting a few people's paper plates. At the door, Viv was stopped by someone. I decided to go find something to drink.

Inside the atmosphere bordered on festive, with people bustling down the hallways, grouped at the stairs, suppressing laughter as their conversation turned from Alice to regular, everyday things and then back again. A little untucked kid ran by. Big-band music was playing somewhere.

I went toward the sound of clatter, and it turned out to be the kitchen. I recognized one of the women from Alice's birthday party, the one with long gray hair, and managed to avoid her by turning toward a table with a large spread on it—meats and cheeses and crackers and a tower of fruit with cherries on the top tier. I picked up a plastic cup of white wine from a tableful of poured glasses, took a few sips, shifted my weight from one leg to the other, and that's when I saw him.

He was blond and young, college-aged if that. A lock of his hair hung away from his forehead as he stuck a toothpick into a roll of turkey. He looked distracted and scornful, until he saw me. His face gave the impression of having been halved and then reaffixed in a slightly uneven way. Ugly and pretty at the same time, the kind of face everyone thinks only they, specifically, can see the merit in.

"The pineapple slices'll blow your mind," he said to me, gesturing with a toothpick. He had a warm, drippy Southern drawl.

I walked to the table. "I'm allergic," I said. "They do this thing to my lips."

"Uh-huh."

"But these are good," I said, picking up an olive and slowly pushing it into my mouth.

"I like how you just did that," he said.

I blushed. "This is a nice old house."

He sighed, looking around. "Yeah."

"You from here?" I sipped my wine.

"Just home from college." He stepped a little closer to me.

"Where?"

"Chapel Hill."

"Let me guess," I said. "Economics."

"History." He stepped even closer.

I felt a twinge of recognition. Had I seen him somewhere before? My mind was blunted by the heat and the wine, and at that point I was still aware of, a little distracted by, the people around us. A man with a cane came up to the table and rummaged through some blocks of cheese, looked at us, and left.

The blond guy reached under the table and fished an empty wine bottle out of the cooler, tilted it toward himself, all business. "You want to help me find the rest of the booze?" he said. I nodded. He walked past me and took my hand.

We went out of the kitchen and down the hallway and out the front door and onto the lawn and he was yanking me through the grass. I didn't have much time to think about all this but I wasn't about to stop it. Then we did a U-turn and went back into the house through the front door, past the stairs and down another hallway and then we were going down rickety wooden stairs into a dimly lit basement. "Have you been here before?" I said when we got to the bottom. "When I was a kid," he said. Then he kissed me.

As this happened, I experienced a kind of slow-release shock at two things: first was how unexpected this whole turn of events was. I'd barely been able to motivate myself to look for the correct shoes under my bed that morning and was picturing a whole day of draining, obligatory, and sad-tinged small talk. The second was how easy this was, how seamless, and how it now didn't seem that outlandish that you could just *meet someone*, at a funeral, for instance. I felt simultaneously exhilarated and frustrated—why couldn't this have just happened before?—by the randomness of fate, and about how some people must just operate on these meridians of luck, going from one precipitous hinge to the next and they didn't even know it, just thought *that was life*.

It was sturdy, by-the-numbers kissing, hot and without adornment. I heard people walking around upstairs. Something crashed to the floor above us.

The rest of the afternoon was like an Impressionist painting—our colors swirling together as we glided out of the basement and out onto the wooden swing, sitting together next to the scattered pink of the azalea bush in the backyard. His smeared red lips and the blush on my chest. Our jazzy flirting with golden, poking saxophone laughter coming through. A mess, a jumble, a crashing, satisfyingly hot afternoon and later we were in a dim, cool living room with carved wooden figures and sheer white curtains and soft shapes of light on the ground.

"You haven't even told me your name," I said, pivoting next to a tall purple vase. This is when I was starting, even though I was drunk, to net the glances people were giving us as they walked by, had, as a matter of fact, been giving us all afternoon, and decided not to care.

"Jack," he said. "Picknell."

It took me a second. That's where I had seen him, in the face of Alice. The resemblance was now striking. He watched as whatever registered on my face registered on my face.

"Let me guess," he said. "You're sorry for my loss."

"I am," I said. "I am sorry for your loss."

"I'm not one of those people," he said, sitting on a footstool, his knees bent in front of him, he took the hem of my dress, "that cares what you say."

I'm still not sure what he meant by this—if he meant that he didn't care whatever awkward construction people attempting to console him used, or me, specifically, that he didn't care what I had to say.

I just stared at him.

"She made it past my twenty-first birthday," he said, "like she said she would." He turned his head and looked out the window at a dry pine tree.

"I—"

"Let's go upstairs," he said, and he got up and took my hand.

It was serene up there. We found ourselves in a bright, renovated room that smelled like paint and polish. There was a red Persian carpet on the floor and a large telescope pointing out the window. I stared at a strange, expensive-looking painting of several bears crowded around a gaslight.

First we pretended to be interested in the telescope. It had felt forbidden to ascend the stairs—that weird feeling of exploring someone else's house. There was no one else up there.

I sat on the windowsill and we made out. We had gotten the knack of each other and it was better, so much better, I thought, than I'd ever had. I flashed to kissing Gerald for a second and became aware of the range of these things, the terrible variegated scale, which means, doesn't it, that it can always be a little better? Or a little worse. But I was having a good time. Not thinking, suspended in a roly-poly dark place, a liquid feeling in my limbs.

He was touching my neck and his other hand was on my belly, then it was under my skirt and in my underwear.

It all felt great—his hand between my legs, the hazy afternoon, the chattering of people downstairs, my chin lifting to kiss him from a better angle.

I'm thinking, It's going to happen. It's going to happen. It's going to happen now, like this, and this is how it was always going to happen. I'm looking over his shoulder for places we could lie down. My mind is racing with logistics: Will I just bend over the computer table? Should we slowly start sliding to the floor? Yes, I've showered today, in case he wants to go down on me. For once, in a stroke of luck, I'm not wearing period-stained underwear. Condoms? Maybe he has one. But who cares? At this point, I'm willing to risk it. Pubic hair? Wild, but there's nothing I can do about it right now. Plus he doesn't seem like the type of weirdly fastidious guy who would care about that.

I wondered in an instant how it was going to be. Was it going to hurt? Would I bleed? Was it going to feel like I would imagine, or be completely different? What was my responsibility physically? How was I supposed to move my body? Were we going to look at each other the whole time, or would our eyes be closed? Were we going to be kissing the whole time, or would he just be surging on top of me? Or should I be on top? What if I gave myself away and he could tell I was a virgin and then wanted to stop? Luckily, something about the way we were together was inspiring enough authority in me that I wasn't actually too afraid of this.

It was all going so fast and it seemed like such a rare window that this would actually happen. He was doing something with his legs, spreading them, with his other hand he was unzipping his pants and then Karen was in the doorway. In a purple dress. Her head was tilted up and her mouth was open.

I went stiff. I said, "Oh." Jack looked over his shoulder and said, "Shit." Karen averted her eyes and said with a forced lightness,

"Your aunt is looking for you." And then there was a deafening pause as we all just stood there. A second went by. A general scramble started. Jack crouched over and zipped up his pants. Karen slammed the door. I yanked my dress down and pulled up my shoulder strap and combed my hands through my hair.

"Sorry," he said under his breath. We continued to straighten ourselves out, to recalibrate. I looked around. The air had gone out and now we were just two unkempt strangers in a room. "No, no," I said.

It's funny how the atmosphere between two people can change so quickly, how ground gets covered that can never be re-traversed. I tried to think of something to say, but the climate had changed. He looked worn out and sad.

What happened next is that we slowly walked out of the room together, in a daze, and down the stairs. We were lightly holding hands, but I couldn't tell if we were *holding hands*, or if it was a left-over remnant of what was happening before. At the foot of the stairs I squeezed his, and he gave me an unsure smile. Then someone called to him, and the doorbell rang, and a woman with red wine spilled on her blouse hurried by, and that was enough to sort of wind us away from each other.

I wandered through the house, trying to find Aunt Viv, who ended up being in the kitchen, and it wasn't long before I was about to leave, closing the car door, scanning the yard for Jack, and we were down the driveway and heading home.

Viv and I didn't say anything to each other on the drive back. I didn't know how much she knew, or if she knew everything; if she was angry at me, or if she was just exhausted and sad. I put my hand out the window and let it glide through the wind. I glided back and forth through my memory of the day as I lay in bed that night. Or it was like I was lying in a boat on a lapping shore, the gentleness and warmth of the world pouring into me.

— *Twelve* —

There was a storm that summer in Durham that became legend-
ary. It came out of nowhere, the sky darkening to a bruisy green
the Wednesday afternoon after the funeral. I'd never seen completely sideways rain before, as if all the water was rushing to get
somewhere else. Once the blasting wind had subsided, the down-
fall came in great reprimanding waves. It was so thick you could
see ripples in it.

Trees were whipsawed and uprooted. There were car accidents,
and power lines went down everywhere. I'd seen bad storms before.
In Texas, we had storms—flat rages that would pummel our tin
shed. But this one was schizophrenic, unsure of what it even wanted
to be, a pressure-cooked whipped fury. Hail drilled out of the sky
from nowhere, and the mangled, cracking thunder was almost
helpless in its anger.

By the time it was over, five people had died when trees fell on
their houses, and two million were without power.

I was driving home from work when it started. When I pulled
into Viv's driveway it was already raining so hard I couldn't see and
accidentally nosed the car into the yard. I ran up to my bedroom to

change into dry clothes and saw that my bedspread was soaked. I slammed the window shut and listened to the panes rattle and the roar outside.

Downstairs I watched the back garden get pummeled, and then went into the kitchen with a giddy sense of danger and watched hail bouncing in the grass.

It occurred to me to worry about Aunt Viv. She usually got home a little bit after me, and so she was probably driving in this mess. I thought of calling her cell phone, but she could be so discombobulated by it ringing that I didn't want her to swerve into oncoming traffic.

We hadn't spoken much since the funeral. I wasn't sure if it was because Karen had told her about what she'd seen or because she was still in a quiet state of grief. All I wanted to do was ask her about Jack. I didn't know exactly what I wanted to talk about, I just wanted her to tell me things, having partially watched him grow up. I hadn't been able to stop thinking about that day. It was like a song I couldn't get out of my head, a memory filled with heavy, drippy gold.

I'd done enough Internet stalking to know that he was on one of the social networking sites I belonged to, and we actually had a friend in common, this girl I'd gone to summer camp with. But I didn't see how I could use that to my advantage. I couldn't look at any of his photographs. I found his name in reference to some kind of tutoring program in an article for the UNC student newspaper. Other than that he was a locked box. I only had that day to go on, to interpret, to keep unfolding like a worn-out treasure map.

I thought, What was implied by our time together at the funeral?

Was it implied by the ease with which we fell together that we were supposed to see each other again and again? Because to me it felt remarkable. Or was there some ending refrain codified throughout the whole thing? I kept tracing it, going over it, looking for grooves or markings that would indicate the genus or species of that afternoon. Or that would give me a plan forward.

A gust of wind socked the house, slamming the windowpanes against their frames. I was just considering again whether I should call Aunt Viv, she definitely should have been home by now, when I heard the front door open and close. I went into the parlor and there she was, completely soaked, hair streaked across her face, her bag crumpled at her feet, and holding an inside-out umbrella. We stared at each other a moment, it seemed that she was about to laugh, and then two things happened, one right after the other. The power went out—for a moment, we were spellbound—and then a loud crash came from the living room.

I said, "What was that?" And we both ran in that direction. One of the French doors leading to the garden had become unlatched and slammed so hard that the glass had broken and fallen out. The door was now lolling open, rain gusting in.

"Don't step on it," Viv yelled as I attempted to roll up the rug the shards had fallen on. She walked quickly out of the room and was gone for a moment, and then returned with some large trash bags and duct tape and we went to work. I held the billowing bags to the door and she secured them, unwinding and cutting the screeching tape. It must have taken us a good twenty minutes to cover the whole thing.

"My God," said Viv as we both stepped back, surveying our work.

The house creaked around us. I'd never seen it so dark during the day.

We set about looking for candles in various cabinets and utility drawers while the wind howled and the world pitched and swayed outside. We gathered and lit them at the kitchen table. Aunt Viv went upstairs to change into dry clothes, and I tried to assemble some sort of dinner for us out of leftovers in the fridge.

At the sink, Viv peeled an apple. The screen in the window was a gray blur.

"You're good at that," I said, watching the skin unwind in a spiral below her swipes.

"Your grandfather was handy with a knife," she said. "He was a whittler and he taught me how to do this."

"That seems grandfatherly," I said.

To my surprise, she laughed. A loud, bawdy guffaw.

I tried to think of something else funny to say. Aunt Viv stole a look at me. "You know you can preorder unpainted walking sticks?" she said.

"What?" I said. "No."

"In case you don't want to whittle them." She motioned with a knife. "I mean, if you want a whittled-looking walking stick, you can preorder them."

"Oh, okay."

"That's how I got started painting them."

"Cool," I said, slightly confused, never having seen any walking sticks around, painted or plain.

She put the peeled apple on the counter, wiped the knife on her pants. "Do you want to see them?"

"Your . . ." I said.

"My walking sticks."

I looked around quickly. "Yes?"

We each took a candle and walked up the creaky stairs to the second floor, to a kind of closetish storage room with lots of random stuff in it. The flickering light threw strange shapes against the walls, and with sheets thrown over certain pieces of furniture, it had the feel of a Victorian ghost story.

"Spooky," I said. "There's lots of stuff in here."

Viv put her candle on a bureau and looked around in an affectionate way. "Yes," she said. "I've been meaning to go through it. I just don't know where to start."

She went over to a cabinet with tall doors. On top of it were two heavy brass bookends in the shape of a man's face with a swirling beard, like Poseidon.

"Whoa," I said. "Can I have these?"

"Um," said Viv, rummaging through the cabinet.

She turned around holding two long, painted walking sticks. One was pink and the other was yellow, and they both had flowers on them, vines, going up and then ending in a burst of petals at the top.

She was looking at me in such a way that it seemed as if her whole perception of this endeavor, maybe of our relationship going forward, would now rest on how I reacted to these sticks. I didn't want to fumble the moment, as I had with her plates, but my instinct told me I should not veer into overenthusiasm.

"Cool," I said, in an inquisitive way, taking one from her. I thought it would suffice to just appear really interested. "You did this?"

"Yup," she said.

"So they're decorative," I said, as if really trying to clear the air about this one thing.

"Yes," she said. "I sold a few, at a craft fair in Franklin County."

"Why did you stop?"

She shrugged in a way that seemed to indicate the whole teeming world of reasons a person would stop painting decorative walking sticks.

"I'll show you something else," she said, taking the stick from me and leaning them both against the cabinet.

I followed her to the other end of the room. She overturned a small metal trash can, sat down, and indicated that I should pull over a stool, which I did. Then, from a different set of drawers she took out something wrapped in cloth. It was a frame, and inside the frame was what looked like a ratty rag.

"I know it doesn't look like much," she said. "But this was one of your grandfather's most treasured possessions."

"Is it some Civil War kind of deal?" I said.

"No, it's Orville Wright's handkerchief."

"Whoa, cool," I said, genuinely impressed. "As in the Wright brothers?"

"Yes, and if you look here"—she indicated a streak in the rag—"that's supposed to be grease from the first airplane that ever lifted off the ground."

"No kidding," I said.

"Can you imagine?" she said, staring into the distance, her face animated and full of make-believe. "Your grandfather, before he sold his business, he owned a few automotive-repair shops. There was one in Kitty Hawk, and he became friends with them through that. He knew them before they were famous, before they were the 'Wright Brothers.'"

"I wonder why Dad never told me any of this," I said.

Viv winced a little, shook her head.

"There!" I pointed to initials embroidered into the cloth, "O.W."

Viv nodded and smiled, pleased.

"You know, there's something of her in you."

I looked up; she was staring at me. "Ellen," she continued. "My sister. There's a resemblance. It's in the way you tilt your head."

"Really?"

Viv nodded again.

We were quiet for a few moments. It had stopped belting rain; now there was just a steady rolling downpour.

She smiled sadly, and looked around.

"This was her old room." She pointed to a corner. "That's where her dresser used to be. A big old white-painted thing."

There was some legroom in the moment, in the air, that I almost thought I could blurt it out: Why are you a virgin? And something about the momentary terms between us would mean she had to tell me the truth.

"So it was a car crash?" I said instead. "The way Ellen died."

"Yes," said Viv. "Just one of those senseless things."

She put the wrapped-up frame back in the drawer.

Something of Viv's childhood came to me then—the hot fields, a father at a sleepy automotive shop, the long afternoons buckling under a sense of grief.

"She'd had a puppy," said Viv. "A little Scottish terrier named

Sandy, who she adored." Viv was playing with a scrap of fabric. "I was visiting you all and we were at the beach once—you were there—at South Padre Island, and I saw a little black terrier, just like Sandy—it could have been her—playing around in the sand. I watched her for a while, and then I watched her run into the water, playing in the waves. I didn't see anyone looking out for her, and I was the only one who saw when the riptide began to pull her away.

"I went in after her," said Viv. "In all my clothes. You know how heavy clothes get when they're wet."

"Wait, what?" I said. I'd been watching the flickering candle, my mind wandering. "You went in after who?"

"The dog," said Viv. "The Scottish terrier. I'd heard about the riptide on the radio that morning. There were orange flags up, to caution people, but of course no one paid attention."

"You just ran into the water? In your clothes?"

"Someone had to. The owner wasn't watching. The dog was getting pulled away. I was the only one who saw it, saw what was happening. It seemed to happen so slowly, and then so quickly. The way the dog was suddenly in trouble."

I remembered that moment with her now: the time-share. The sense of trouble in the air. Something to do with Aunt Viv.

"What happened?" I said.

"Well, it was a big ordeal," said Viv. "A lifeguard had to save us both." She laughed. "My shoes and skirt—I was wearing sneakers for some reason, they were so heavy in the water. I think I overestimated what I would be able to do, and I got swept away by the current, too. Your parents weren't happy. Well, they were confused, mostly, I think."

"What happened to the dog?"

"He was saved. A little girl claimed him, I heard. I never met her."

"Sheesh," I said, after a moment.

Later I tried to picture it: a bright day, her skirt billowing around her in the water. I could feel how it would be, with the waves and world wheeling around you, your clothes and shoes dragging you down as you fought the sea. Would most people have done that? Was she insane? I couldn't decide. It had sounded so logical, the way she put it. But who would go fully dressed into the ocean after a stranger's dog? It occurred to me that Viv might be one of those slightly unhinged people who, if she'd been born in a different era, or was present at a certain joint of history, might have distinguished herself as a warrior queen, someone capable of displaying unwieldy bouts of bravery at the right time. The light flickered against her face. For a moment, outside of everything, I felt a belt of affection for her, and for her strong, crazy stripe of honor. She played with the edge of her shirt, lost in thought.

We got up and put away the walking sticks, then went back downstairs and made dinner out of leftovers in the fridge. The lights came on, but only much later, in our sleep.

The next morning I e-mailed Jack. I tried not to get too hung up on the wording or the tone, because I knew I would never send it if I did. I composed what I told myself was a breezy message and pressed Send.

I looked out at the bright trees. The sun was beating down on the back garden, the hydrangeas already hanging their puffy heads.

Jack. Jack Picknell. It didn't seem like the right last name for him. Picknell implied something sterile to me, pettily bureaucratic and tucked in. And he was all craggy warmth, blades of light slicing out.

Here was my opportunity to lose my virginity in a situation where I actually wanted to, where I wasn't forcing it, the noose of time tightening around my neck. Here was something where the normal wheels of attraction, so ever present with other people, were there for me, turning the proper way. It could be a simple, unassailable, all-American summer fling. Maybe that's what I would say to my daughter fifteen years from now. "It was a summer fling." I'd leave out the part about us meeting at a funeral and me being twenty-six. But the whole situation with Jack had the possibility of reframing my plight—I just lost my virginity to some guy I met one summer, like the kind of person for whom things fell into place like that, one fortuitous event hooking onto another until I was wearing a big floppy sweater and staring out at the waves before having understanding sex with my husband and reflecting on our lives that were ladled with the perfect amount of happiness and well-proportioned, surmountable problems.

If he would just write me back.

I tried to get on with the rest of my morning. That afternoon I sat in the arctic cool of the office, in my swivel chair, waiting and checking my e-mail, and the day continued like a can being slowly wrenched open.

Jeannette came by at one point, swishing up to my desk in one of her beachy, floral numbers, her gray hair blow-dried into its usual apotheosis, and told me a story about how she'd contracted her son-in-law to repaint their kitchen, but he'd made a real cock-up of it, her words, and spilled paint all over the marble countertops. "A little dab'll do ya!" she said, cracking herself up.

This was just the kind of conversation I would normally try to draw out with her to prevent me from having to work on whatever assignment I'd been given. Jeannette had been there for decades, and so her seniority, in combination with her salty personality, made her pretty much unassailable in that office and no one ever messed with her or, by extension, the person she was talking to.

But I was so distracted by waiting to hear back from Jack that all I could do was offer the necessary nods of agreement and incredulity when required. She finally floated away.

At a certain point, to route myself from staring at the screen, I actually took the initiative of dusting off the crystal clocks. That took all of twenty minutes. I sat back down and checked my e-mail and my heart fell. Nothing yet.

I swiveled to the minifridge and got a minibottle of water and savagely twisted the top off and was about to start tearing off a bunch of warrant-in-debt sheets from a thick pad when Elliot appeared at my desk.

Sometimes it's as if we're all operating together in a collective consciousness where we just know, implicitly, some things about another person without being told. Or maybe this thing with Jack happened to coincide with whatever sea change in my favor was already happening between me and Elliot, in our dynamic. But he was nervous, solicitous, in a slight posture of rejection even before we'd said anything to each other.

"Hi, Julia," he said. He was holding something in a brown paper bag. His hair was tied back in its daily ponytail and looked greasier than usual. His smile was overeager.

"Hi," I said.

"I brought you this." He started carefully trying to withdraw something from the bag he was holding. I had a feeling of dread about what I knew was now going to happen, and wished terribly that I could go back and prevent this series of events from being set in motion—that I would never have given him a gift and compelled him to return the favor. That I could have just trusted the summer to bear up an appropriate suitor, as it had with Jack, who eclipsed Elliot in every way, and showed him for what he was all along: a stranger, a middle-aged fluorescent-lit guy at a law firm with whom I was now and then forced to interact. He was having a lot of trouble withdrawing this object from the paper bag. He was stooping over it a little, trying, it seemed, to reach his hand down and scoop something from the bottom without upsetting the packet at all.

It was a little cactus. A little office cactus. The kind with old-lady hair coming out of it, surrounded by pebbles in a small red pot.

It was way off base, and I now had an inkling of the feeling Elliot must have had when I gave him the sandscape and he must have wondered just who the hell I thought he was that he would possibly be appreciative of such a thing. But then the more I thought about it the more I realized that this cactus actually fell pretty squarely into the persona I'd endeavored to project about myself—someone vaguely interested in Southwestern shit.

I smiled and said, "This is really cool," with what I hoped was the appropriate amount of warmth and authenticity, which was really hard, like putting on a wet bathing suit.

"You could put it on this prime real estate," said Elliot, pointing at a gap at the front of the desk between Jeannette's calendar and a jar of pens. I think he meant for what he said to be inflected with a little bit of self-deprecating humor, but then somehow the moment became very grave.

"Yes, I could," I said, and we both watched with great seriousness as I slowly pushed the cactus, a few paper clips caught in its wake, into the gap on the desk.

I stared at it for a second too long, and then looked up at him and smiled what must have not been the right smile—"Did you get it at the ol' cactus emporium?" I said—because he now seemed a little resentful, as if this had not gone at all like he planned and he was sick of the whole thing and wanted to minimize any fallout by just getting on with it and going up to his office.

"No. Nope," he said. "The nursery. On Ivy Road."

"Oh, okay," I said, nodding deeply, as if this was filled with really interesting texture and shading. "Well," I said. "Thank you. I really like it a lot. It gives this desk a more laid-back feel."

He laughed, and then nodded, and then turned around to walk up the stairs, only to bump into Allison, who was on her way down, spilling some papers she was holding. He bent down to help her pick them up.

None of this really mattered to me, though, because when I turned back to my computer I saw that Jack still hadn't written back.

It was three o'clock. I had two and a half endless hours to go. I rummaged around for some candy I might not have found before. I opened and shut the desk drawer to see how much force it would take for the paper clips in a little compartment to slush over. I practiced making a suction cup sound on the desk with my hand. I sighed, got something caught in my eye, and the truth was I really just wanted to start my *life* over.

After work I stood in my bedroom, in my underwear, in an unshowered, humid torpor. I'd come home in a black mood and lain facedown on my bed for an hour. Then I'd called Grace.

"It feels so rare, you know? That that would ever happen." I'd told her about him, the reception, everything. "That you would ever actually just meet someone. It's like, oh, okay, this is possible."

"But just because you meet someone— I know it's kind of thrilling that you hooked up so fast—"

"Think about it. Think about all the people you meet, the guys. I know you're with Chad, but, most of them. Talking to them, it's like, this immobile, fluorescent-lit conversation, and it does not pave the way for— Nothing would ever happen. So, to have it happen so fast like that, it means something. It means it works. There was some mechanism there."

"We are talking about a twenty-one-year-old, remember?"

"If that."

"Just because you guys kissed in a shed—"

"A basement. And then an office."

"Doesn't mean there's some inherent special thing there. He's a college guy. He was attracted to you. You were drinking and he was emotionally distraught and you hooked up. Simple as that."

"But it's not that simple."

"I'm not saying he won't write you back."

If it didn't work when two people crashed together like cymbals on a summer afternoon, and then couldn't stop talking to each other, then when would it? I had a vision of the bright grass underneath the swing Jack and I were gliding on. My hands were sticky from wine I'd spilled. He'd separated a lock of my hair and placed it in his mouth.

"You have to remember," she said, "his mom just died."

"I know," I said.

I was trying not to let my voice tremble with emotion. Everything was hanging by a thread. I'd been yanking the pull cord on the summer and this was the only thing that had caught and I couldn't imagine going back to, where?—Arlington? Texas?—without having accomplished my goal, and what was I going to do? I thought of myself sitting in another office. Get a job showing people houses? Make my own jewelry?

I pawed at a rug on the floor with my foot, trying to get a wrinkle out.

"Did I tell you about my mom and dad?"

"No, what?"

"They're getting separated."

"What?"

"I know."

"Hilary and Doug?"

"Yup."

"Why?"

I sighed. "I can't really tell. I think they're just— The way my mom puts it, I think they've just grown apart."

My parents used to entertain a lot. My mom wore these blue button earrings. I had the clearest picture of my dad pouring a boozy drink from a pitcher into her glass, she's laughing, her hair soft and curly and graying around her face, he's looking at her with admiration, as if she's just said the most perceptive thing in the whole world.

"Jeez," said Grace.

We were quiet for a few moments.

"How are you doing about it?" she said. "I mean, how do you feel?"

"I spoke to my dad," I said. I put my hand in my wet armpit and looked out the window. "He sounded, I don't know, it's hard to explain. Different. Like there was this slant to his voice I'd never heard before. It's like I could finally see him, the way anyone else would. He's a charming, slightly wayward man."

"It is weird when you can see your parents from the outside like that."

"Yeah."

"What about your mom?"

"I don't know," I said. I walked over to the bureau and looked in the decorative pitcher. There was dust and a dead bug. "She's rewriting the story," I said. "She says now they were never content, but I remember, they *were* happy."

"But you can never know."

"No."

My whole childhood—me playing in the backyard, my parents hard at work on their computers in their messy office, the supplies closet I'd open sometimes, because I liked the smell of new plastic folders and erasers, and I'd waver there, sucking it in. I saw us all from the outside—our house in our flat neighborhood, but I saw it on an incline, a slant, so that we were sliding, ever so slightly, so that we couldn't even tell until we were flying off the edge of the earth.

"What are they going to do?" said Grace.

"My dad's going to stay with some friends in Miami for a while, and my mom is going to take care of things with their business. They're thinking of selling it now. She's in a different mood every time I talk to her. I can't tell if this breakup is a new thing, or if there was something there from the beginning. A thread."

"Things change," said Grace. "Everything changes. Everything sloughs itself off, renewing the surface, until there's nothing there from before."

We were quiet for a few moments.

"Can I tell you something?" said Grace.

I always pictured Grace the same way, the way I remembered her from college—with a faint mustache, and her brown hair slicing along her shoulders, and her face tilted in reflection at a soapstone sculpture at the university museum.

"Yes."

"My whole life—I've never told anyone this—my whole life, all the men I know, my dad, my brothers, Chad, everyone, I've always felt sorry for them. From the get-go. Even when I was a kid. Just a kind of ancient, inherent sadness for them."

"Yeah," I sighed. "I kind of know what you mean."

I sat on the edge of the bed and then lay back, stretching my body so my legs hung off like dead weight.

"I don't know," I said. "It still doesn't make sense to me. Maybe one of them is having an affair or something."

My parents and Jack. Two suppurating questions, hanging in the air. Two things that would never be solved.

"Or maybe they really did just drift apart. Maybe it's that simple. Things usually are."

"No, they're not," I said. "They're usually really, really complicated."

Viv was at the kitchen table, wearing a blouse with a pattern of palm leaves on it. She was poring over her little leather notebook and also had some large pieces of paper spread out in front of her. It struck me how her weekend or casual clothes all looked like they were bought from a gift shop in Key West. Her hair was carefully parted and resting behind her shoulders.

After getting off the phone with Grace, I'd wandered down, determined to distract myself.

I went over to a cabinet and rummaged around until I found a small tub of beef jerky. I yanked the top off and withdrew a piece and then turned around to face Viv.

"I like your shirt," I said, chewing.

"Thanks," she said in a distracted way.

"It's really relaxed."

She looked down at it.

"It's like"—I hoisted myself up onto the counter—"beach time!"

"Yes," Viv said, and jotted something down.

"I'd like to go to the beach," I said. "I haven't been in years. Not since I lived in Texas. The last time I went, there was a wedding, and the wind blew away a bunch of linen bows . . ."

She was in the middle of a project. There were lots of pieces of paper arranged in front of her, and it looked like she was making some kind of graph in her notebook.

"What are you doing?" I said.

She put her pencil down and looked at me directly. Then she sighed and sat back. "I'm trying to map out my show," she said. "But I'm having a hard time with it."

"Why?"

"Well, I don't have a lot of space. Everyone gets a certain allotted wall space." She tapped her chin with her pencil. "And I'm not sure what pieces to use."

"Well, they're all really good," I said unhelpfully.

"Thanks," she said uneasily.

"I'll need your help," she said, "if you don't mind. I'll need help getting the plates to the center, because I'm going to have to pick up some things after work, and I won't have time to do both."

"Sure, yeah," I said, and nodded. And I kept nodding, as she told me what I was going to have to do, and how it was all going to work, but all I could think of was my e-mail. And how I wanted to check it. And of Jack, and all the things he did—like how he'd taken that bottle of wine out of the cooler and sort of tossed it up and caught it again. So confident. So at home with things. And that's how it would be with me. He'd manhandle me in an affectionate way all the time. He'd toss my hand up when we walked down the street, and I would be included in the easy, confident way he had of owning everything that was around him. Everything would be ours if we were together.

"But it shouldn't be too hard," Viv was saying, "because I'll have all the crates packed up and ready to go, waiting for you in the living room."

"Sounds good," I said.

But when I thought about my e-mail I got this doomed feeling. I put down the tub of jerky and stared out the window above the sink. The day was thick and humid, and outside was an anguish of lush greenery.

"It'll be great," I said.

I felt hot, claustrophobic, deranged. I kneaded my palm.

"Yes," said Viv. She anxiously turned her watch around and around on her wrist. "Yes."

— *Thirteen* —

When I saw Jack standing next to the wide plastic leaf of a fake palm tree, I realized he was one of those people who looked a little different every time you saw them. This time his face looked almost pretty—strewn blue eyes, ruby lips.

I had finally, finally gotten an e-mail from him, four days after I'd written, asking if I wanted to meet him at the restaurant where he worked, a place called the Lazy Parrot out on Route 29, at five o'clock that same evening. It was the day of Viv's art show. The reception was from seven until nine thirty, and I was supposed to ferry the plates over there after work. She'd wrapped them up carefully and they were waiting for me in the living room. I decided I'd go and get them first, then go and meet Jack, and go from there to the McCormick Center, arriving at six o'clock. Viv would be setting up the platters of hors d'oeuvres she'd taken it upon herself to provide. Then we'd hang up the plates together. I would have plenty of time.

Back at home, after leaving work early, I quickly shoved aside the maps and jumper cables and old books that were in my trunk to make room. I carried the crates that were waiting for me in the living room down the porch steps and then hoisted them into the car. My hair got in my face. My armpits were prickling. I checked my watch.

I got in and drove off only to sit in unexpected traffic for fifteen minutes. I stared at the shimmering tar roof of a pancake restaurant. By the time I got to where Jack was, I would only have about half an hour before I would have to leave to get to the center in time. Maybe I could be a little late. Viv had, in my opinion, overestimated the time it would take to put up the plates anyway.

When I arrived, I immediately realized there were a number of things at odds with the laid-back island vibe the restaurant was trying to project: the scalding sarcasm with which the high-school girl at the entrance was passing out leis, the aggressive air-conditioning, the flat-screen televisions projecting a cage-fighting competition, and the handful of twentysomething men below watching it with an itchy air of aggression.

I was glad I'd brought a shawl. I stepped out of my shoe, which was stuck to the sticky floor mat. The lei girl was writing the specials on the whiteboard and pointedly not turning around to greet me, and then there was Jack, by the palm tree next to the host stand, looking, I got the distinct feeling, as if he'd forgotten I was coming.

"Heeeeeey," he said, overcompensating, greeting me as if I were some college buddy. "How's it going?"

"I'm good." I nodded.

"Cool. Cool," he said, and looked around the restaurant. "I'm glad you caught me. This is my last night here."

Caught him. As if he hadn't had nearly a week to respond to my e-mail. I had to hide my disappointment by rummaging through my bag for some ChapStick. "Mmm-hmmm," I said, using it liberally. "Great. Me too."

He regarded me with a look that at the time I had a hard time deciphering. But later I knew what it was—the troubled expression of someone in over his head, who had bitten off more than he could chew, but knew that if he just tolerated it for a little while it would be okay.

"Thanks, Chelsea," he said to the lei girl. And then to me, "You want a drink?"

I nodded.

We walked down an aisle between booths. I slid into the one he pointed to, and he went to the bar. I stared at the starfish tapestry on top of the table. I flipped through the huge laminated menu and wondered what was taking so long. I looked over to where he was standing with his friends and tried to identify by their postures or demeanors if they were talking about me.

It was like slowing down five hundred horses, but I forced myself to regain some measure of composure. It was purely survival. I couldn't stand it to let my center erode and sit there all vague and dispersed.

But when he sat down, I wasn't some paragon of poise nor did he immediately have the upper hand. It was all somewhere in between, both of us toggling between different versions of ourselves, glinting and dimming, trying to intuit where to give or take, what the stakes were, what the other person expected.

Whatever had happened at the funeral was there again, or at least some slight part of it. It wasn't just the fleeting alchemy of that humid afternoon, I was grateful to realize—we actually liked each other. He was looking at me fondly, almost despite himself, as if there was some essential part of me that universally tickled him. There was something there, I knew it.

"What are you doing?" he said.

"I'm reading the ingredients in the drinks," I said.

"They're just drinks."

I felt delighted.

"Are you aware," I said, "that you have a drink on your menu that's basically got a piece of pizza in it?"

"The Crazy Mary."

"That's what it's called?"

"It's got cubes of cheese and pepperoni."

"Why would you order something like that?"

He sat back and affected a faraway gaze and a raspy voice. "People come here to escape."

I laughed. "Are you doing an impression?"

He looked happy.

"I'm being steely," he said.

"I thought it was someone specific."

"It was, sort of," he said.

"I'll have the Zeus," I said, pointing at the menu, when the waitress came. She looked at us knowingly and then left after Jack ordered a beer.

"You sure about that? The Zeus?" he said.

"You don't think I can handle it?"

"You ever seen the movie *Cocktail*?"

"Who was your impression of?"

He sat back. "This guy," he said. "This old man that ran a lodge we would—my family—would stay at in Alaska sometimes in the summer." A shadow passed across his face. Was he thinking about Alice? Later, when I reframed the whole night with that—that he just lost his mom—it all made more sense. The guy was a frayed cord, a jagged edge. But the other thing was that under the grimy stained-glass lamp of that restaurant and in that weird situation, we were still both actually having a good time.

"He was always saying these indecipherable but ominous things," he continued, playing with a straw wrapper. "He'd be like, 'Gray skies this morning, sure to spit on a goose's wing.'"

I laughed.

"Or like, 'Wind is up, kiss a squaw.'"

"What does that mean?" I said.

"Anyone's guess," he said.

I don't know how we got onto the subject but we were discussing what it would be like to be stranded at sea and how we would both react to the situation. And he said something I didn't expect that really threw me. He said, "I've always known that in a situation like that I would be the one to freak out or jump overboard or something." The guilt on his face brought the conversation to a halt. It was obvious he'd said something he felt was true, something he'd thought about a lot. When I turned over this statement, it was all wrong to me. It seemed to negate everything preceding, everything buoying him and me and this whole night and all the unacknowledged assumptions we had about each other.

"No," I said, with too much conviction, "you wouldn't be like that."

He looked through the window and into the blue-lit parking lot. His smile guttered out a little. I watched him, and a fear rose around me, I didn't know where it came from, that he was going to be rudderless and unhappy, going through life. That he was going to be a sad man. I tried to shake it off.

My drink came. It was in a huge plastic cup, the kind of thing you would take to a baseball game, filled with blue liquid and green ice cubes and swirly straws and a few little umbrellas.

"Holy God," I said.

"I told you," he said.

"Is this even legal?"

"It's for sorority girls," he said. "They like to order it to impress us with how, like, adventurous they are."

"You shouldn't say stuff like that to me," I said. "I'm not the kind of woman who doesn't like other women."

"So you like sorority girls?"

"I don't not like them," I said. "I don't really know any."

"Well, I know a lot."

"I'm an enigma, I guess," I said, after a moment.

"An enigma wrapped in a huge scarf."

"It's a wrap," I said.

Now and then he would draw back a little and I could feel what he was doing. It was all too much, and it wasn't the right time, and he didn't want to get involved with this twenty-six-year-old woman and her complicated wrap. She was probably always cold. She would be needy and critical at the same time and he could see himself doggedly following her through a mall holding a bunch of shopping bags while she bought a ton of bath beads and acted insane, and really, he just didn't have time for all this. Or maybe he was too young to envision all of that, but I wanted to tell him that it wasn't like that. I wasn't like that. And it didn't matter how old I was and also, what was going on right now, as we were talking, how easy it was—that was actually pretty rare. It didn't happen that often between two people and he needed to grab on to it while he had the chance and it's tragic the way so often the things we want are presented to us before we're ready, before we can recognize them for what they are.

We were talking about pets: "The reason I don't like cats that much is because I can tell that if they were just a little bigger they would try to kill me," I said. By this stage there's a high red in both of our cheeks. Now and then I get the sense by the way he laughs or the way his eyes go all liquid, that he's never actually talked to a girl before for an extended, connected amount of time, or never really had a good time doing so.

I told him about a cat I had named Smoky who was killed in a car accident. He told me about a turtle he got when he was ten.

"Kitty," I said, "another cat. Feline leukemia."

"Brownie, a hamster," he said. "Death by fucking boredom, I think, I don't even know."

"Birdy, a parrot. Flew away."

"Georgie, my mom's poodle. Still kickin' it."

"Cleary, a fish, neglect. I was ten."

"Cleary?"

"Yup."

"Why Cleary?"

"He was see-through."

"You're really killing it with these pet names," he said. "You are trouncing it."

"Well"—I shrugged—"I'm glad you can recognize genius when it's just staring you in the face."

I'd made about five inches of headway into my blue drink and I was just on the knife's edge of being drunk and I decided to slow down, because I didn't want to tip it all over the edge. I knew there was a fine line between being pleasantly freewheeling and careening into red, ugly bombast. Also I still needed to drive in a bit. So I took it down a notch and started sipping my water. I peered back outside at the lot. I looked down at my phone. Two text messages from Viv. Jack was telling me about a kayaking trip wherein he found a gold watch. This segued into a story about how his stepfather was a dick. I then told him about my friend Katey, who lived down the street from us in Texas, and who had an evil stepmom who would make us walk very slowly down the hallways because she didn't want the pictures lined up on the walls to fall askew.

I said I'd be right back. In the bathroom (sticky, cold, dirty clumps of wet toilet paper) I found that my face was a little more red than I thought, and I had the beginnings of some hive-like splotches on my neck. I checked my phone again. Now there were two missed calls from Viv. I had to leave. I would be late, but some plausible excuse would be enough. We'd still have time to hang the plates. Maybe Jack could come with me. Then, afterward, we could go and get another drink.

But back at the table, he had a funny expression on his face. "You want to go to this lake I always used to go to," he said, "when I was a kid?"

"A lake?" I said. "Right now?"

"Yeah, you're a swimmer, right?"

"Yeah, but I have— There's something I have to do."

"I used to go there all the time in high school," he said. "It's not far from here. Remember where Karen lived? There's this creepy old ice-cream shack. We'd swim out to the water filtration tower, or whatever it was, in the middle. We could race, me and you, to the tower."

"I mean," I said, "I will beat you."

He smiled.

"No, it's just"—I wiped my palms on my dress—"I can't really. I have to do this thing. I promised my aunt. She has an art show, at the McCormick Center?"

"It's really secluded," he said. "There's a little beach area. I haven't taken anyone there since high school."

Under the table, he put his foot on top of mine.

We stared at each other.

My phone buzzed in my hand. Viv again.

"Who is it?" he said.

I looked down at it. Secluded lake area, I thought. I liked the weight of his foot on mine, and I wanted to keep feeling that weight and to never stop feeling it, and it seemed preposterous that I would be the one to cause it to do so.

"No one," I said, and turned it off, and put it in my bag. "Is it close? The lake? Should we go?"

He leaned back and smiled. "Yeah," he said. "Let me just get my stuff."

Then we were walking through the hot parking lot toward his

car, a beat-up green sedan. Inside it smelled like weed, and there was trash on the floor. "Sorry," he said, as I kicked away a balled-up paper bag. "It's fine," I said, laughing. We pulled out and started driving on Route 29, out toward Cismont, and then took smaller, overgrown roads. The sun hadn't gone down yet, and the warm, dusky air seemed to shimmer with magic dust. The trees, the ivy crawling along the power lines, a faded and half-burnt billboard for an old zoo, the sound of the cicadas, it was all humming with possibility. His hand was on my leg, sitting there like a frog. I didn't want to move, didn't want it to hop off.

Viv's face swam through my mind, but I pushed it away. I would make it up to her. Maybe this guy, Pete Wexler, would still be here tomorrow. Of course he would. I would personally take the plates to him, wherever he was. It was all going to be fine. I pictured Viv in the center, looking around anxiously. Something tugged at me and I felt a little sick. But then I took that picture and put it in a box, and put that box in the back of my mind. The alcohol helped, it helped swirl it all away. For now I just had to rest my hand out the window while Jack's hand rested on my leg, and stare out at the orange sky, and keep shimmying myself into the opening the night was giving us.

We drove in a comfortable, anticipatory silence. It had been about twenty minutes when Jack said, "Uh-oh," looking at his dashboard. "We are out of gas." I hadn't seen anything in miles. "There's a place coming up," he said.

After a minute we pulled into an old station with a busted sign and car parts strewn around the lot. In the shop there was someone at the cash register, leaning back, his feet up on the counter. "You have to pay cash first," said Jack. "I'll be right back."

"Sure," I said, and then watched him go up to the store, swing the door open. I looked to my other side. The trees across the street were filled with darkness. A streetlight flickered on. I watched a pickup truck pull up to the pump in front of us. A man without a shirt hopped out and walked into the store. A child with lank blond hair stared at me from the back window.

Jack was behind a rack of newspapers. Then he walked to the back where I couldn't see. I looked down and straightened my dress and stared at my nails. I put my hair up, then took it down. After a few minutes, the man without a shirt came out and shook some candy at the kid in his truck. The kid laughed and soon they were gone.

I shifted uncomfortably. It had been fifteen minutes. Without the wind coming through the windows the heat was close and stifling, and I felt beads of sweat forming at my hairline. I opened the door and stepped out of the car. I walked across the lot and went into the store: fluorescent-lit, sticky cold air-conditioning, a few bags of chips on the dingy ground, fallen from a rack. A teenager sat blankly at the cash register. I looked around and saw Jack next to the ice machine in the back. He was standing with someone taller and roughly his age.

"Oh, hey," said Jack as I approached. "Sorry. This is Scott."

Scott was tall and had small, dark eyes and looked at me dismissively before turning back to Jack.

"So then JJ is like, 'Let's firebomb it,'" said Scott. "And he lights a firecracker and drops it in. And all the fish are like—" Scott made convulsing motions as if he was being electrocuted.

"Oh, shit!" said Jack, covering his mouth, laughing.

"You should have been there." Scott reached into a glass case and pulled out a hot-pink energy drink and twisted off the cap.

"Tzzzz tzzzz tzzzzzzz," Jack said, shaking in the same way, imitating Scott's electrocution.

They both burst out laughing.

Jack's whole bearing was different. His hands were deep in his pockets and he was hunched over and there was a mean glint in his eyes.

Scott had turned away from me just enough to indicate I wasn't included. He took a swig from his drink.

"So you're gonna be there tonight, right?" he said.

Jack's eyes cut to me for an instant. "Yeah," he said. "Definitely. Wouldn't miss it."

"I don't know," said Scott, putting his hands up, defensive. "Ever since you went off to that big fancy college . . ."

"I know, I know," said Jack, affecting a deeper Southern accent. "All right," he said quickly, starting to back away. "Munger Road, right?"

"Yup, yup," said Scott, pointing to Jack as we walked away. "Munger Road."

We went out of the store together, Jack now walking with a swagger he hadn't used before. I got into the passenger side and he pumped gas and got back in and started the car all without looking at me. He shifted gears and we peeled out of the lot, going back the way we had come.

"Wait—where are we going?" I said.

"Change of plan," he said.

"What is it?"

"I haven't seen that guy in forever!" He slapped the steering wheel. He glanced over at me. "But, there's this party, and I kinda have to go." He was walled up, far away.

"Really?" I said. "What about the lake?"

A ripple of discomfort went through him. "I have to go to this party," he repeated. "I'd invite you but it's just a bunch of old friends."

"So, we're just not going to go? To the lake?"

"It's not that great anyway," he said.

Grand, majestic disappointment. An ocean liner sinking lusciously into the sea. I looked down at my lap. I felt scatterbrained and jittery. Jack sat forward, sat back. He turned on the radio, turned it up loud. He fished around behind him and withdrew a baseball cap and put it on. Readjusted it on his head.

"I . . ." I started.

"What?" he said, and then looked back at the road, ignoring me.

Back in the parking lot of the restaurant, I pointed to my car and he pulled up next to it. We sat there for a few moments. "Well," I said.

"I just haven't seen those guys in a really long time," he said, still gripping the steering wheel, staring straight ahead. He finally looked at me, and for a second it seemed like he was back to his normal self. But then his face clouded over. "Take care," he said, and then took out his phone. I climbed out and had barely shut the door before he zoomed off.

In my car, outside the restaurant, I stared at the patchy grass on the concrete divider in front of me. It was dark now, and across the highway you could see a construction site, plastic sheeting billowing in the breeze. For the first time in my life I wished I had a cigarette, something to do with my hands. A jeep pulled up next to me, and three laughing women got out, all wearing heels. They stumbled toward the restaurant. I dug my fingernails into the worn padding on the steering wheel.

The night whittled down in my mind, and I had a moment of clarity—I was never going to see Jack again. He wasn't going to solve my problems, and I knew what I had to do. I fished my phone out of my bag and turned it back on. It vibrated with messages, but instead of checking them I brought up my e-mail. I typed the words that were streaming through my mind and pressed Send:

> Dear Elliot,
>
> Could we make an appointment for you to fuck my brains out?
>
> Very best,
> Julia

I turned on the ignition and started driving. The night swirled around in my head as I pulled onto the highway. I passed a megaplex movie theater, some car dealerships and empty parking lots. I felt like I was filled with a jumble of blocks and I didn't know how to get them to fit together. It was eight thirty. By the time I got to the McCormick Center it would be nine. That left half an hour until the reception was supposed to be over. We wouldn't get to hang the plates, but at least Viv could show them to the guy from Southern Imports. I would make up an excuse, car trouble, something like that.

My eyes settled on a red sign in the distance with a kicking boot—the Boot Warehouse—and then a thought occurred to me that nearly stopped my heart.

I needed my phone.

It was in the backseat where I'd flung it after sending the e-mail. I twisted around to look but didn't see it. A few seconds later I wrenched around again and flung away a parka, and there it was, next to an empty water bottle. After reaching back a few more times, almost swerving into oncoming traffic, I was finally able to grab it. My hand shook as I brought up my e-mail, and a dizziness that was hot and cold at the same time came over me as it was confirmed: I'd sent the e-mail to the whole office.

I stared at it, my face burning.

And then it all happened so fast—the peal of a car horn, then another. I looked up to see white flashes, cracked light, the side of a turquoise van. There was a terrible jolt from behind, screeching brakes, and the sickening sound of breaking glass in the back.

For a moment, all was still. I was in the middle of an intersection, and the cars around me were positioned crookedly, as if everything had been shaken up and then settled in the wrong way. Slowly, it all started moving again, the cars straightened themselves out, someone honked at me; it blared and blared well after they'd passed. I continued through the intersection and pulled off to the shoulder. The plates, I kept thinking. The plates, the plates.

It must have been two or three minutes before someone knocked on my window. My hands were shaking as I rolled it down. I saw a gray woolen cardigan, the kind that cinches at the waist with a belt. A woman's small, pointy face lowered. She had short, spiky hair and was holding a phone.

"Are you okay?"

"Yes," I said. I brushed some hair out of my face. "I think so."

She looked quickly around the inside of my car, noticed the phone in my lap.

"You were texting."

I didn't say anything. Her fingernails were painted purple.

She sighed, straightened up, cinched her cardigan. "Well, look, do you want me to call the police?"

I saw her car parked behind me, the hazard lights blinking.

"Are you okay?" I said.

She looked really angry now. "You realize you ran a red light? You could have killed someone? How old are you?"

"I'm—"

"Look, what do you want to do? My car is fine, a few scratches. Do you have insurance?"

I pawed at the glove compartment. Some candy wrappers and a mini-umbrella fell out. Lights kept tracing by, cars on the highway. When I looked back at the woman, she was texting, shaking her head in disbelief. She cinched her belt again and looked at me. "Well?"

Standing at the edge, the lake looked like a wide, raggedy black hole. Along the shore were swaying reeds, and the night roared with crickets and frogs. It was so loud when you really listened to it, I thought. Something plunked in the water. I was in a small beach area, just like Jack had said. I'd climbed over the chain-link fence he'd mentioned. And to my right, I could make out the outline of the dilapidated ice-cream shack. I looked around. A car drove by behind me, in the distance. The hair stood up on the back of my neck when I thought I heard the crunch of gravel, like it was coming my way. But I must have imagined it.

After exchanging information with the lady in the gray sweater, I'd gotten out of the car to look at the damage. There was a large dent on the right back door, and when I opened the trunk it revealed what I already knew would be there—because of the hasty way I'd packed the crates, because I hadn't taken the time to arrange things so they could lie flat, they'd tipped over. Most of the plates had fallen out and broken. I stared at the shattered pile. I picked up a shard and looked at the meticulous gold trim, now dusty with white powder.

I'd pulled back onto the road and kept driving. But instead of going back into town to the show, or heading back to Viv's, I turned around and went the way Jack and I had gone, toward Cismont, toward where Karen lived, toward where the lake was supposed to be. I passed the faded billboard for the zoo, and the gas station. Even though it was dark now, it wasn't hard to find the turnoff Jack had mentioned. There was really only one small, scraggly road it could have been. I drove down this road, through low foliage, the path getting narrower, until I came to what looked like a parking area.

I stepped back from the waterline and pulled my dress over my head, and left it in a pile along with my shoes in the sand. I wondered how deep the lake got. Where it dropped away under you, and whether it was man-made, or what kind of creatures were breathing rapidly in the prehistoric depths at the very bottom.

The hotel room I stayed in after the trials in Tallahassee blinked into my mind, as it often did at the most random times. There were wet towels on the floor. The smell of coconut hand lotion came from the bathroom. My roommate, Cissy, was outside, on the balcony, her feet up on a plastic chair, telling her parents all about it on the phone. She'd made the team. I was sitting against two overstuffed pillows, my face chlorine-tight, not feeling. I was floating above it all—there was a show on the television, a stern-looking female lawyer said, "The winter palace is the only place"—and trying to determine where it had been, the silent hinge where I'd ceased being an Olympic-class swimmer.

The truth is I hadn't even come close. You had to be in the top two. I'd been eighth. It was incalculable, what that meant—the vast difference between your assessment of a situation and what's actually possible.

But maybe I hadn't tried as hard as I could have. Because now, pushing off the sand—the water was lukewarm, even in the night air—I felt I had tectonic strength in my shoulders. I started swimming toward the filtration tower I thought I could see in the distance, just like Jack said. The sound of the cracking plates replayed in my mind. What I wanted was to reach that place where you've obliterated yourself with exercise, where a seam comes apart and it all goes blank, where I wasn't imagining Viv's face as she checked her phone, called me, tried to buy time. There was no fathoming the utter mess I'd made of the summer, the nuanced and majestic ways in which I'd ruined everything. I wanted to get away from all that thinking as fast as I could. To that place where you're only pushing because of some primordial, flickering electricity—whatever it is that makes humans go.

I swam probably faster than I'd ever swum in my life. Or maybe it just felt that way in the darkness and splashing, locking stroke onto stroke and getting farther away from the shore. I swam down, and the water closed above. I clawed toward the bottom, going deeper and deeper. I saw myself from the outside, making a diagonal line toward the center of the earth, going through all the sedimentary layers, putting leagues between me and civilization. Then I pictured my lungs, two straining, bright wings in the darkness. Then inside out, far away, inner-ear agony. I swam back up. At the surface, I looked around, gasping for breath. I was in the middle of the lake. There was no tower. It was completely quiet. I could have been suspended in space.

I pulled up to the shore, and coughed, and lay there. The water lapped against my feet. I closed my eyes, and eventually went to sleep.

— *Fourteen* —

When I opened my eyes it was still dark, and I couldn't tell if it had been five minutes or five hours. I was freezing. The sand, which had been so inviting to sleep on before, was now cold and itchy. I sat up and pulled my knees to my chest, letting my eyes adjust. There was trash I hadn't noticed before, a plastic bag and a crumpled soda can, lolling at the shoreline. A bird gave a mournful call. Back in the car, I saw that it was five in the morning. I'd slept there for seven hours.

As I drove home, and approached the fields surrounding Viv's house, I realized I hadn't been up this early since my swimming days. Sometimes it had been torture to wake up at that hour, all wrong, like combing hair against the grain, but I now realized that I missed it—the pink sky, the secret, cathedral feel of the morning.

I parked and walked up the stairs to the house. I thought I'd just go up to my room, avoid Viv since she'd be asleep, shower, and fall into bed, but then I heard a sound, a chair scraping. I walked down the hallway, and there she was, awake, in the dim kitchen, sitting at the table. She was wearing a bathrobe. Her hands were clutched around a cup of tea. Her hair was bedraggled around her shoulders, her eyes were red, and her lips were pushed to the side in an awful way.

"I'm glad you're okay," she said, bringing the tea to her lips, without looking at me. "Although I wish you'd been in touch with me earlier in the night."

"Viv," I said.

"There was a good turnout. Everybody came, like they said they would. The catering was beautiful—did I tell you I decided to have it catered at the last minute?"

"No," I said.

"It was expensive, but it was worth it to me. I said, 'She'll be here,' when Pete kept looking at his watch." She glanced at me. "Incidentally, we have three platters of deviled eggs, olive canapés, and chicken skewers with peanut sauce in the fridge in the basement."

I couldn't move.

"When he showed up, I was so embarrassed, so anxious. I think he could tell. He was such a nice man. He stayed much longer than he had to, walked around and looked at some of the other art. Of course, I was still hoping. I was still thinking, here he was. I was still thinking, things could be different now." She looked into the distance; her chin quivered. "If Julia would just arrive with the plates. In the end, he ended up talking to one of the other women. She does stained glass. And he liked her stained glass. He liked it very much . . ." She trailed off.

Outside, the sky was starting to turn purple. The room had a surreal, suspended quality, with the light beginning to shift. I felt sick. When the silence became unbearable, I said, "I had to run an errand, at the last minute, and I was just coming back, and I got hit from behind, at a light." My voice sounded high and false. "And my phone ran out of battery. I couldn't call anyone."

"The plates?" she said quietly.

I shook my head.

Viv didn't react. Finally, she said, "Your mother called. You'll want to call her back. I think she got a little worried when I got in touch with her last night trying to figure out where you were."

With that, she got up from the table and walked to the sink with a definitive air, as if ending the conversation. I watched as she rinsed her mug, put it in the dishwasher, and then started fiddling with the dial, which had always been a little wonky. She cursed at it under her breath. Not knowing what else to do, I turned and began walking away, and then it came—her voice, with a wild, guttural quality. "Why?" she bellowed.

I whipped around, half expecting her to be hurt, missing a finger. But she was fixed on me, rage hammering.

"Why?" I said.

"Why is this here?"

I couldn't see—she was looking at the side of the fridge. She reached for something and showed me, a *National Geographic* I'd put in a magazine holder attached there.

"I—"

"Why don't you put them back?" she said. Her voice climbed in a strangled way. "Why don't you put them back where they belong? You leave them on the coffee table in the lounge. You take them out of their place in the sunroom and leave them, and it's the same with other things, books; you want to read something of mine—*fine*—but why don't you put them away? You must have noticed—who do you think puts them away? Do you think they walk themselves back to the right place? Every single time I pick up after you, and then you do it again. I find them on top of the fridge, on the stairs, you left a stack on the piano, not five steps away from the proper place, and on the porch swing in the rain. And how you dig your toenails into the coffee table in the sunroom? And chip at it?" She was yelling, her face in disarray. Her bathrobe had fallen open and gaped inelegantly at the chest. "I've *seen* you do it and now it's *ruined*." At this, she slammed the magazine back into the holder, which broke off the fridge and clattered to the floor.

My mouth fell open. She put a hand on the counter to steady herself.

"You're loud," she said grimly. "Do you have any idea how loud you are? You slam every door, and you leave your things everywhere. It's not appropriate, when doing laundry in someone else's house, to leave your underwear hanging on every surface." Her voice was climbing again. "The way you slam up the stairs without even saying hello, and you've been in my studio, I know you have— looking through my things, and that ambush with Gordon, and the way you acted at the funeral." Her voice cracked and she put her face in her hands. Her back shuddered a little bit. A few moments passed. When she looked up, something had deflated.

"The way you carried on with Jack," she said, wiping her nose. "None of us could believe it."

"I didn't," I said; my face was hot, my throat was thick. "You don't understand."

"I'd seen you flirting, but I didn't think you would ever— He's practically a *teenager*. His mother had just *died*." She looked directly at me. "You were ridiculous. You were drunk."

I wanted to run away.

"It wasn't just me, okay?" I said. The words erupted. I wanted her to know that, I wanted to get that point across.

"It doesn't matter," she said. "You were my guest, you should have known better."

"I know."

"You're twenty-six years old."

"I know that." It came out more petulant than I meant.

"What were you doing in my room?"

"What?" I said, stricken.

"There are things— I mean, were you just snooping?"

"No." Yes. "I was looking for cotton swabs." I was trying to find out about you. I was trying to understand how you became the way you are. And the more and more I've found out, the less it adds up. You make no sense at all. You're water flowing in all directions. You're a different person every day. Sometimes you even look different to me. There'll be a masculine slant to your nose and chin, or you'll be guilelessly pretty. I've tried to find out about your whole life and I haven't found out anything, and we haven't become friends, and this summer is a frayed cord hanging in the air, and the mystery of you, the great mystery that I have not been able to figure out and probably never will—why have you never had sex on this earth?—is still hanging in the air. And nothing is guaranteed. And why haven't you been able to be happy? Why haven't you had this thing? When does the scale tip the other way for you, and what are we supposed to do with this kind of unfairness? And could it happen—that your life could go off, in subtle increments, and end up bombastically wrong—to anyone? And what if you *want more*? What about what you *want*?

"Cotton swabs."

For half a second, I thought about telling her everything. Why I'd acted the way I had that summer, what was behind my spastic behavior. Maybe she'd understand. Maybe all our misconceptions about each other would collapse into a shared heap.

Instead, I said, "Yeah." My voice cracked. I pushed down a sob. "Cotton swabs."

Aunt Viv squinted, and for a brief moment she looked sorry for me. She steadied herself against the counter again, and then walked back to the kitchen table and sank into one of the chairs.

We were both quiet. The clock chimed. Six o'clock.

"I had to meet someone. An old friend was in town," I said, absurdly, my voice high-pitched and warped. "And I really thought I'd make it back in time with the plates, for the show. And then this car hit me. I ran a light."

Aunt Viv was nodding, short little efficient nods as if I was confirming something she already knew, as if I was confirming something that had long been confirmed about her life. She put her face in her hands again. When she looked up, her eyes were wet, and she started talking without recrimination, just, it seemed, explaining.

"Ellen was the history buff," she said, "not me. She was the one who became interested in legend, the Knights of the Round Table and all of that. I only became interested in it later. I think I wanted . . . I only wanted to carry it on for her. She had a teacher.

Mr. White. And she was going to study history. It was just an exercise, to be close to her again. The King Arthur plates, I wanted
to do something she would have liked."

I slowly nodded my head.

"She always used to read me the same part of *The Once and Future King* . . ."

After a moment I said, "They were beautiful. I could tell."

Her eyes were shining. "You think so?"

I nodded. And we were quiet like that, for a while, suspended, it
seemed, in a ragged silence. I slowly sat down across from her. I
said quietly, "I thought you liked him."

She looked up.

"Gordon," I said. "I thought, maybe, if I could just set you
up . . ."

"With just *anybody*?" She shook her head and went back to her
own thoughts, a palm against one of her eyes.

We continued to sit there. My fingers pressed themselves into a
beaded coaster that was on the table. I knew if I got up, and looked
out the kitchen window, there would be a layer of mist. Soon, the
trees in the distance would start to cast long shadows over the field.

"Aunt Viv," I said. She turned toward me. I swallowed. "Why are
you a virgin?"

She stared at me for a moment. She took a deep breath. I saw
something flicker in her face, and then she exhaled and said—and
I found it extraordinary not just because of what she said but because of the way she said it: "I don't know." She said it mournfully,
with a deep well of helplessness. *I don't know*, as if it was a question
that had plagued her her whole life, still did, a deep wound. A ques-

tion that was indeed in the air, I could tell by the way she didn't question my questioning; worth asking, worth answering, that she had asked it of herself her whole life because it was confounding and *didn't* make any sense.

She looked at me. "I tried," she said. She nodded to herself and dabbed an eye with the collar of her robe. She turned her head the other way, and dabbed the other eye, and then stared out the window above the sink. A minute passed. I didn't think she was going to continue, but then she said, "There was a man. Richard. He was my boss at the hospice, where I worked for such a long time." She pulled her robe tight, wiped away her tears again as they came, smoothed down her lap. "We were really good friends. We worked together beautifully and, in a way, became really close. We had lunch together, just the two of us, three days a week for eight years. He was unhappy in his marriage and I guess I always thought . . . I don't know what I thought." She looked around the room. "I saw him recently," she said, glancing at me. "At the grocery store. He was there with his wife and his son. It was as if there had been nothing between us. Maybe there never was."

"But, what about before that? When you were younger, there was never . . ." I wasn't sure how to continue.

"I was religious." She slowly shook her head. "And it was different back then. You waited. And so, I waited. I was here a lot, helping with the house, with your grandparents. Someone needed to. I couldn't just leave them here alone, with Ellen gone. And your father, he just"—she shook her hand dismissively—"went off." She touched her ear as if making sure it was still there. "I couldn't just leave them.

"I was never one to"—she looked down, she was trying to straighten the collar of her robe—"throw myself at someone. And then I said to myself, 'Don't *expect* so much.'

"I tried," she said, almost to herself. She dropped her hands into her lap. She looked at me. "In my way, I tried." Then she smiled a smile that was resigned and filled with sadness and sympathy and brimming with her whole gorgeous array.

For a moment, it was like I could see it all, finally—Viv, lit like a sunrise splashed across the sky, every filament of her, the exact torn way in which she was gorgeous. She was strong, strange, gifted, forgiving. I knew, with a pain, that she would forgive me. I knew, in a way, she already had. What she'd seen and understood about me this summer I'd never know. But she had seen it, and forgiven me for it and I hadn't done her the same service. I hadn't seen her whole. I wanted to tell her, so badly, how much I admired her. I wanted to tell her how I'd had it all wrong.

Instead I watched as she rose and walked unsteadily out of the room. Outside the window the sky was turning a lighter purple. For the first time, I realized there was a chill in the air.

I got up and I caught her just as she was about to go up the stairs. "Aunt Viv," I said. She stopped but barely turned to me. "About the plates. About last night." She winced. Her lip quivered. Finally, hotly, it surfaced inside me. "I'm so sorry. I'm so very sorry, about everything. If I could go back—I would do anything. I would do anything to be able to go back." She hesitated for a moment, and then continued on her way up, and into her room.

— *Fifteen* —

"This is Pete Wexler," said a man on the other end of the phone. I could hear traffic in the background. I pictured a short man, in a white linen suit, wearing vintage buttons on the lapel, staring into the dusty window of an antiques store.

After Aunt Viv went up to her room, I sat at the table for a long time. The house was silent, as if nothing had happened. Slowly, by grades, the kitchen filled with morning light. I went outside to the car and opened the trunk. I hauled out the crates of broken glass and put them on the front porch. I carefully took out the dusty pieces, one by one, and laid them on the floor.

"My name is Julia Greenfield," I said.

"Yes?" said Pete, in a slightly hassled tone. Blaring atmosphere on the other end. It sounded like he was in rush hour in Hong Kong.

"I'm the niece of Vivienne Greenfield," I said. "From last night, with the plates."

"I'm sorry?"

"The McCormick Center," I said. "Last night? You went to see Vivienne Greenfield's plates?"

"Yes, okay."

"I'm her niece."

A siren blared and then receded.

"Look, what can I do for you?" he said.

Not every single plate was broken. And some of them were only in two pieces. As I laid them on the floor, I realized it wouldn't be that hard to put some of them back together, if they'd cracked in a clean way. I could see the new series that Viv had been working on, the Knights of the Round Table. They were all in dappled, colored shards, but when you put them together you could imagine how they would have been. The plates had a gold trim, and cursive writing on the bottom. They depicted knights in detailed finery sitting on their horses, women in pastel dresses dancing around a maypole. There was one of a row of hanging flags against a gray brick wall. And one of a field, dotted with wildflowers, in front of a castle. They were all in Viv's childlike, measured style.

Now, pacing in my room, talking to Pete Wexler, whose number I was finally able to track down, I had a bad feeling in my stomach. In the bleating light of day, the feeling of what I'd done was not going away, not at all. It was humid, and the floorboards creaked as I walked around. I knew if I opened the window I would just let in hot air like a dog's breath.

"It was my fault," I said to Pete Wexler. "I'm the reason she didn't have her plates. I got into an accident and didn't show up."

"Well . . ." he said, unsure, impatient.

"And so I'm calling because I wanted to see if there was any way— Are you still here in town? Or if you could come back. Or if you'll be back in this area anytime soon."

"If I'll be back in Durham?"

"Yes."

"Well, it's possible. I'm not sure."

"There's got to be a way for you to see them again. Have you seen her website? Last night couldn't have been the only chance."

"Yes," he said. "Possibly. I don't know." A car horn. Someone shouting on the street.

"If you come back—we'd love to have you for dinner. We could show them to you, or . . ."

But he was saying something. ". . . maybe relocated to another store, we're expanding, so I'm not sure if I'll be touring the South again next summer. But we're always on the lookout. Look, do you— Is there anything else?"

"Oh," I said. "So—wait."

"Because I'm in the middle of something here. I really have to go."

"Okay. Okay."

"Have coffee with me" is what the e-mail from Elliot, which I received later that night, said. I stared at the screen for quite a while. The truth is that I was already formulating a plan.

I hadn't gone in to work since I'd sent the e-mail, and hadn't received any phone calls from the office asking where I was.

After talking to Pete Wexler, I'd called a few other home-goods and decorative-arts stores, asking if they were interested in a local artist's work, if they sold things on consignment, but I hadn't had any luck. I'd gone back out to the front porch, and on a different part, laid down some newspaper. And then I hunched over the pieces of the plates and tried to put back together what I could with superglue. I was able to salvage the one of the cliff in the ocean, a few of the Wild West ones, and three of the Knights of the Round Table series. A few more came together. They had seams going down them where they'd cracked, but it wasn't too noticeable. By the end, standing back, I saw that there were enough for some sort of display, some sort of show. I'd get them put up somewhere. There could still be an event.

When I got the e-mail from Elliot it fell into place. What I needed was someone who knew about local art galleries.

He suggested we meet at five o'clock the following afternoon, at a rooftop restaurant that overlooked the marquee of an old movie theater. When I arrived, there were tall potted plants in the corners and a couple of old people in linen shirts drinking wine. I pulled an aluminum chair across the concrete.

"I'm so sorry about that e-mail," I said as I walked up to him, before I could lose the courage. He was sitting in the sun, in a relaxed manner, squinting at me.

"It's fine, it's fine," he said, putting his hands up in a placating gesture.

"I don't know what I was thinking." I sat down and put my bag under the table.

"I admire you," he said. He was smiling, like he was happy to see me.

"You do?"

"People don't usually do stuff like that."

"Really?" I said. "You don't get e-mails like that every day?"

He laughed. "Let's just say you've given Jeannette something to talk about for the rest of her life."

I looked down at my plate. It was shaped like a seashell, or a palm frond. I couldn't tell.

I said, "I don't want people to think— I thought I'd e-mail them, Kramer at least, and tell him that there was never anything between us. That you never did anything like that. I don't want them to assume . . ."

He looked anxious; he was shaking his head.

"No, no," he said. "You did me a favor."

"I did?"

He sighed sadly. He looked to the side. "Yeah," he said. The waiter came with two glasses of water. It was quiet for a few moments. He turned back to me. "I've been divorced for two years."

It took me a second. "What?"

"That's what I was trying to tell you."

"Wait, you have?"

He moved his chair forward. "When it was all going down, I didn't want to tell anyone at work—you know how people talk. Just for a little while. I was going to, I really was. Then I just never did. I kept wearing my ring to keep up appearances, and then it just seemed like too much effort, almost, to take it off. And so, I didn't really know how to say that. To you."

I looked out over the rooftops. "You're not married," I said slowly, almost to myself. A train passed below us. The roar of it drowned out my thoughts. I listened to the steel grind, the high gritty whine. On a rooftop in the distance an old woman beat two outdoor chair pillows together. When I looked back at Elliot he was studying me.

"I'm sorry," I said. "I'm sorry you had to go through that."

He exhaled. "It's okay." He looked tired. And older. He had a small gold clip on his tie. I pictured myself putting my hand on his stomach.

"So you had to tell them after my note," I said. "I blew your cover."

He laughed uncomfortably. "I didn't *have* to do anything. It's none of their business. But, yeah, I thought it was a good time to come clean."

"What did they say?"

"Oh, you know." He made a dismissive gesture with his hand. "No one *says* anything."

For a while we just sat there. I was in the sun. I looked at the horizon. I touched my hair and my hair was hot.

"I don't know," he said. He sighed. "I've been in Durham for a long time now. Might be time for a change."

Slowly we began talking about other things. I told him about Vivienne's project, about how excited she was for her show, and the car accident, leaving out everything about Jack, of course. And how I wanted to make it up to her.

"I think there's usually more of a process," he said. "As far as I know, you have to apply to get your work displayed. But I'll ask my friend. Sure, of course I'll ask her."

I exhaled. "Okay," I said. "Okay, thanks."

I ordered five glasses of fizzy water. No alcohol. We talked about the office. I told him about my swimming career. I asked him how he'd ended up in Durham.

"It's where Devon wanted to move," he said. "She went to grad school here. I just sort of haven't left yet." He flickered with sadness.

"Oh, okay," I said.

We stood outside the restaurant, both squinting, not sure what to do. He looked at me quizzically and said, "Do you want to come up to my apartment? I live just over there. We can look at the data. From the radio telescope."

"No, I can't," I said, thinking I should just get home, and that there wasn't supposed to be another chapter with Elliot, not after everything that had happened, that I'd done. "I've got things I have to do." I turned around and started walking away. A moment later I looked back. He was still standing there, staring at me.

It was mesmerizing. The blown, scattered lines of light coursed down the wide flat screen. Every ninety seconds they slightly changed their grain. You were supposed to sift for something out of the ordinary. Something that could qualify as unusual. Something that could be anything other than our world's rote buzzing. Something that could mean an inquiry, an actual out-of-this-world head nod from another civilization. I've never been one for alien stuff, but sitting there for a moment, with Elliot explaining it to me—anyone could be the first person to intercept this signal, which would be the biggest discovery of humankind—for a second I believed, I watched. I searched for something outside myself.

I'd turned around and gone back to Elliot and said yes, on second thought, I'd like to see the radio data. We'd walked to his apartment, his blazer slung over his briefcase. He was right, it wasn't far, just a couple of blocks away, and upstairs in an old yellow building. I flashed back to Gerald, driving me miles out of town in his silent car.

It was a long, open-plan apartment, with wooden floors and lots of natural light. We put our stuff down and Elliot went to the fridge to get us a drink. I walked around, looking at things. The fastidious cleanliness of his office seemed to have carried over—nothing was out of place and even the art books on his coffee table were stacked with precision. There was a watercolor painting of an Indian chief with a colorful headdress made of streaks and feathers fading into the sunset as if the whole sky was a part of his finery. There was another of the chief contemplating some pyramids in the distance. I studied a triangular porcelain vase with some glass stalks sticking out of it.

"That's my ex-wife's," said Elliot. "A lot of this stuff is."

"Oh, okay," I said thoughtfully, and decided to leave it at that.

He had a hand towel slung over his shoulder and was holding a bottle of champagne.

"Want some?" he said, wrapping the towel around it.

I looked at my watch. "Really?"

"It's the only thing I have to drink."

I thought about it for a second. "Sure."

"I'm not trying to seduce you, and this has nothing to do with your e-mail," he said.

"Cool!" I said, starting to blush.

We went over to the sofa in front of a large flat-screen television that was attached to a laptop on the floor. He turned off the lights and shut all the blinds until it was as dark as it could be during the day. He came over and sat down next to me and switched it all on. Vertical dashes of light, a Serengeti of them, filled the screen.

"How does it work?" I said.

"It's picking up electromagnetic radiation," he said. "All those specks you see, they represent radio signals from, just, satellites, other planets, broadcasts."

"Other planets?"

"The wavelengths they give off. Every object does that, to an extent."

"Okay. So that's not the sky."

"No, no. Well. It's just data. From a huge radio telescope, the one I told you about, in California? It's picking up signals from things that are in the sky. So what you're seeing is a kind of vast amount of indifferent, clashing reverberations."

I nodded.

"What we're looking for, waiting for, is something that's not random. Something that signals intent and meaning. It would take the form of a straight line, or two lines, down the center. Something targeted. A pattern. Something trying to reach us."

I sipped from my glass and stared at the screen. "Got it," I said.

Elliot leaned back in the sofa and nudged his shoes off and then put his feet on the coffee table. He sighed. "So yeah," he said. "This is pretty much what I've been doing since my divorce."

I laughed. I sank down into the sofa with him. He took my hand. We watched the screen. We were like that for about ten minutes, and then he kissed me. Just like that, we were kissing.

The feeling of staring at the screen, the roar of the universe, was still in my head. I felt him being cautious, and I thought it had to do with the e-mail—how he'd known that I sent it in some addled state, and probably hadn't really meant it, and so he really didn't want to be seen as taking advantage of all that. I knew that if this was going to progress in any way beyond kissing, I was going to have to be the one to sanction it. I wasn't quite sure how.

But then he blazed over all that by putting his hand up my shirt. It felt good, all of it—the tilting feeling of the champagne, the silver glow of the screen, the oceanic warmth of the moment.

I pulled away and said something I'd been meaning to say. "I have to pee."

"Okay," he said, wiping his mouth. There was something very intimate in the torn tissue of that moment, and that's when I realized that it wasn't just actual mechanical sex I'd been missing out on, but this feeling of free-falling trust, of liking someone and having them like you so much that there was no end to the liking.

When I got back we commenced a heavy-breathing make-out session wherein I felt like I was on a swaying rope bridge. Elliot smelled like cedar, or like the attic in someone's mountain house. A little creaky. But there was another scent there, a kind of behind-the-ear, unwashed-hair him-ness.

"Do you have a bed?" I said.

His bedroom. I stood there, in my socks, while he went to use the bathroom. I wondered if I should take the socks off. There was a fish tank with swaying plants. His bed was really big and had a smooth gray comforter on it. I thought, I'm going to have sex in this modern room next to a fish tank, with or without socks on. There was a bookshelf with lots of fantasy and science fiction paperbacks, all very neatly arranged and alphabetized. I stared at his digital clock. Was I going to tell him I was a virgin? It's not like I felt I couldn't, or that I thought he would balk or make me feel weird about it in any way, but I knew that saying something like that could change the current—add a hiccup that might throw the whole thing off.

My instinct was not to say anything. I kept staring at the digital clock. He came back into the room but I didn't want to turn around.

He put his hand on my back and we started kissing again and then we sank down onto the bed. I tried to make sure the pace was sustainable, that it would continue at a good clip. Riding a bike, swimming, keeping it all up, up, up with the right balance of moving parts.

Just do what he does, I thought. That's a formula you can follow. He took off my shirt, and then I took off his shirt. He kind of gathered me into himself and I held on to him. He took off my shorts, and I started fumbling with his belt.

Then we were completely naked—two naked adults, with the air-conditioning hitting our private parts. He turned onto his side and propped himself on his elbow and looked me up and down, which I didn't like very much. "A swimmer," he said. "A swimmer's body."

"I'm a virgin," I said all of a sudden. And I realized I told him because I felt about to hang glide off some precipice alone, and I really didn't want to be alone. I wanted someone to be there with me—a friend. I wanted Elliot.

"Really?" he said. "Well, I'm a Unitarian."

I grinned. It was a stupid joke.

He fished a condom out from somewhere and put it on and lifted himself on top of me and said, "Just let me know if anything doesn't feel right." But I knew it was going to hurt, and it did hurt.

It hurt a lot. But then the pain subsided. I realized which way was up and got my bearings. I kissed his neck. He laughed a disbelieving laugh—his voice cracked and it felt special, to hear him that way, and I got a sense of his outer reaches, like the sun hitting the sea far away and you can see all this distant surface area.

I then thought of a movie I'd seen at a friend's house when I was a kid, where two people in rugged jean jackets were having sex against a red Porsche in the desert. It just flashed through my mind.

Here's something I appreciated: that Elliot wasn't being so sensitive or mincingly polite that he wasn't enjoying himself. He sighed really loudly when he first went inside me, and it was not at all horrible to watch the raw expressions cross his face.

It seemed to go on for a long time.

"Here," he said, and he turned us over so I was on top of him. "Some girls like it better this way."

"I can't tell if I do," I said.

"It's a lot to take in, all of this," he said, looking a little sweaty.

"Yes," I said.

"Okay," he said, and then we were back in the first position, with me on the bottom. "Do you mind if I . . . ?"

"No, no," I said, "go ahead."

He came inside me.

He lay down to the side. I was lost, in between channels of white noise, but not in a bad way. The sheets were wrinkled and my pubic hair was wet and there was a drop of semen on my stomach.

"Look," I said, pointing to it.

He propped himself up on his elbow. "Yup," he said. "That's America."

I stared at him. There was so much I didn't know about this person.

"Do you want me to touch you?" he said.

"What? No," I said. "I don't know."

"Don't worry," he said, resting back on his pillow, looking up. "You'll learn. You'll learn what you like."

I looked around. I slowly drummed my fingers on my stomach. I picked up a paperback that was on his night table. *"The Afternoon Planet,"* I said.

"It's a fantasy book," he said, "part of a series I'm reading. It's a little too . . . I'm not sure if I'm going to finish it. I'm all for empire and rebel shit, but sometimes these books get a little too heavily militaristic, with battles and battles and battles."

I put the book back. By the little bit of sun I could see through the blinds, I could tell the light outside was getting all ripe and late-day.

I thought of other moments I'd gotten something I desperately wanted: when I qualified for the Junior Nationals when I was thirteen; the phone call about my full scholarship to Arizona State; even when I was a kid—this certain kind of gourmet chocolate egg I was allowed to eat only on Easter; in fourth grade, when Shelly Goodall finally realized, exactly when I wanted her to, that, because she'd ruined my Advent calendar, I was the one spreading rumors that she once French-kissed a prairie dog at Epcot Center.

Elliot was looking at me playfully. He was still him—I still liked him. I was still me. I should have known not to worry so much about any of it, about all of it. But I would never have been able to not worry.

"What should we do now?" I said.

"I've got some ice cream. Do you want to go up to the roof?"

"Yes, that's what I want to do."

So that's what we did. We sat on the warm tar roof and ate soupy ice cream. We talked about what it was like for him to grow up in Allentown, Pennsylvania. And about my parents and Costa Rica and Texas. We talked about the office, and about Jeannette, and what was up with his ancient secretary, Caroline. "She's just a nice old lady," he said. The late-day sky billowed pink, and below in the street, restaurants started to get crowded and lights turned on and twinkled in the distance. I felt frayed, wise, and alive.

"You know what I've always been interested in?" I said.

"What?" He was sitting cross-legged. His shirt was on inside out.

"Medieval stuff. Like, the Black Plague and all of those kings and queens, the Wars of the Roses and things like that. Catapults and wheels. Braveheart. You know what I mean?"

"Yes," he said.

"I want to learn about all that. The Yorks and the Lancastrians. All of that stuff." I readjusted my position, shifted so I was leaning back on my elbows. "I feel like I never really got an education. I wasn't really paying attention."

"Maybe you should study history," he said. "Go back to school."

"Yeah," I said. "Maybe. I guess that's something a person would do."

"You could do anything," he said. "You're young. You're lucky."

"I couldn't be more lucky," I said.

— *Sixteen* —

You think you'll be different. You always think you'll be different. But then normalcy quakes and breaks the ground beneath you and takes over. And then you're just you, like you always were, on a hot day.

It was a week later. I was standing in the warm, sunny upstairs gallery of a bookstore in a town called Sperryville about twenty minutes from Durham. "Can someone tell me where to put this vase?" I said, looking around. Elliot came up the stairs holding a crate of wineglasses. He put it down. "Last one!" he said.

"Is the wine— Should we bring the wine? . . . Hi, excuse me!" I said to a teenage guy wearing an apron who had just trotted down the stairs from the roof. "That vase, do you know where it goes?"

He put his hands up helplessly. "I don't really work in this part," he said, backing away.

A grim lady in a turtleneck was packing up her exhibit of clay pots. She was sitting on the floor, surrounded by crumpled newspaper. I was supposed to be putting up Viv's plates, but everything had taken longer than expected and we were running late. I went over to the lady, who was slowly wrapping something in tissue paper. "Is that vase"—I pointed—"is that part of your display?"

"No," she said. "Mine are examples of traditional Apache wedding—"

"Okay, well, do you know where the manager is?" She just looked at me. "Maybe he can help. I was told you'd have all of your stuff out of here by four."

She straightened up and said indignantly, "My friend is supposed to be here any minute to help."

"What about that?" I pointed to a box of decorative antlers. "Is that yours?"

Her eyes narrowed and she was about to say something when I felt a hand on my shoulder. I turned around. Elliot. "I can help you move it," he said. "The vase. We can put it in that back corner, by the radiator."

He'd come through and gotten me an opening here, his friend's gallery. When I'd first seen the space, it looked perfect—wooden floors and big windows letting in lots of light, and plenty of blank walls to hang the plates. But I hadn't realized it would be oppressively hot in the afternoon because the windows were painted shut and the air-conditioning wasn't working. I was disheveled and sweaty from all the crates we'd brought up the stairs, along with the boxes of wine and wineglasses, some chairs, a few tables, and a cooler. There were lines of chalk on my dress. My makeup was running down my face. There were boxes and newspapers and crumpled things everywhere. Elliot looked at me searchingly. I breathed in quickly. "Okay," I said. "Let's just move it." As we turned to walk in that direction, my knee hit a stool and three wineglasses wobbled, fell, and broke on the floor. I looked around frantically. Everything was dusty and coming apart.

Two hours later, I stood talking to Viv's friend Karen. "It is," I said. "It really is important to have good posture." After we'd moved the vase, I went to the bathroom and washed my makeup off. Then Elliot and I helped the turtleneck lady clean up her stuff quickly, and then we slowly hung Viv's plates with brass hangers. We put everything out—the wine, the glasses, jars of fresh flowers. The hors d'oeuvres had finally arrived from the catering company. I'd spent most of the money I'd saved that summer on the event. It looked good—not exactly like I had pictured but still nice. But it was too stuffy, and Viv had come too early. She was standing by herself, looking cool and unencumbered, wearing a long ivory skirt and a tunic, a little satin scarf slung over her arm as she held a glass of wine and looked at the display.

"Excuse me," I said to Karen. Elliot was coming up the stairs. I went up to him. "I want to introduce you," I said.

"Aunt Viv," I said, a moment later. She turned around. "This is my friend Elliot. He helped me set this up. This is his friend's gallery."

She looked at him, slightly bewildered. His hair was out of the ponytail, flowing down and around his shoulders. He was wearing a purple shirt, like a magician would wear.

"Oh, hello," she said, in the voice I imagined she used when talking to a salesperson.

We'd been exceedingly polite to each other since the episode in the kitchen. I'd told her at one point that I was going to leave two weeks early, after the show, essentially, and she'd nodded quickly without really looking at me and returned to her book. I could tell she was still angry, but it was almost like she didn't have the energy for any real vitriol and so was just tiredly indifferent. Even when I told her about the show itself, she'd been polite, but I got the feeling she was humoring me. She'd dismissed me, the whole summer, and was just waiting for it to shove off and be over.

I'd invited everyone I could think of, all her friends, people from her job, Gordon. I'd asked the local newspaper to put a mention of it on their website. I wanted her to walk in and see people admiring her plates and be quietly delighted. Muslin curtains would ripple picturesquely in the breeze. Maybe it would even be better than the original reception would have been. She would feel healed. The afternoon would suture whatever had been ripped between us, and we would both leave feeling sage and replete in our newfound friendship and lessons learned.

But now we stood in a tense circle. Me, Elliot, Diane, Karen, and Viv. No one was drinking. The hors d'oeuvres were untouched. Everyone was glancing around nervously, not sure what the center of this was supposed to be, when what was supposed to be achieved was going to be achieved. The weight of it all was snuffing out any spontaneity or ease. There was a terrible silence until Karen said, "It's wonderful, Viv, it really is."

And it really was. I hadn't arranged the plates into their original groups, because so many of them were missing, but rather put them all together in a sort of patchwork. Some of them had gold trim, some of them had the cursive writing on the bottom, explaining the scene. I felt that whenever I looked at them, I noticed something different. This time, it seemed that they were created with an off-kilter sensibility, as if there was an inherent strangeness to them that made you want to keep looking.

"Thank you," Viv said. An employee on the lower level of the bookstore erupted into a coughing fit. The door squeaked open, and we all looked in that direction, hoping it would be someone coming in for the show, but it was just a man leaving. I could tell Viv was feeling burdened, because not only had her previous opening been ruined, but now she had to persevere through this tortured gesture where everyone looked at her with fragile smiles.

"Eat!" I said. "Please, everyone, have something to eat. There's so much food."

We wandered over to the food table. Elliot put his hand on my shoulder in consolation. Then two strangers came up the stairs—an older couple. The man was tall and stooped and wearing a leather vest. The woman had a pixie face and bright white hair and said, kindly, "Is this the Vivienne Greenfield exhibit?" I could have kissed her.

"Yes!" I said, and motioned around the room. "Welcome."

They floated over to the plates.

Twenty minutes later I stood talking to a large bald gentleman with thin wire glasses.

"It's a great organization," he said. "Once they had a fund-raiser—who could paint a chair in the most creative way! You could sponsor an artist. One person painted it to look like a cow."

"Cool," I said, looking around. There were more people now. A few more of Viv's friends had come. I watched a woman stroke her hair as she talked to Diane. A group from the bookstore had wandered up, probably attracted by the free wine and food, but they were looking at the plates. Viv was talking to Gordon. I'd been really surprised when I'd seen him and had avoided eye contact. Viv gestured with her hand as if she was measuring an inch. He laughed. Maybe their friendship couldn't be characterized by that one interaction at the restaurant. Maybe the old cells of that night had sloughed off, and a new skin was generating underneath.

"It was on peach schnapps!" said Viv's friend Diane, a little later.

I was talking to her by one of the windows. She had a red wine mustache. She was telling me about the first time she'd gotten drunk.

"Ha!" I said. "I think for me it was the Amaretto at the back of my parents' liquor cabinet."

"No!" she said wildly. "We were in a *library*. It was actually very *serene*. There were marble *elephants*."

I had no idea what she was talking about.

More people had trickled up the stairs. There were many different conversations happening, and there was just enough chatter, enough sporadically erupting laughter, to lend a sense of activity and festivity. I said goodbye to Elliot and went back up and started gathering plates and empty glasses and crumpled napkins. I looked over at Viv. Her cheeks were red. She was motioning with her arms. Someone tapped her on the shoulder and gave her a card. She seemed pleasantly pulled in all directions. An image would stay with me—Viv, pointing something out on one of her plates, tracing a line with her pinkie finger, her eyes generous, engaged, her face knitted with the strain of trying to explain something, nodding, showing off a little but also wanting everything for you.

I stood outside the gallery, thanking people and saying goodbye. The small town we were in seemed to be made up of one main street and nothing else. After a series of shops ended, there was nothing but fields and trees and power lines in the distance. Viv came out, talking to a stranger. They said friendly goodbyes and parted ways. She had her bag and was ready to go, and it seemed that she was going to walk right by me, but she stopped there and gave me a resigned smile. "Are you all packed?" she said, folding the small satin scarf she'd been wearing.

"Pretty much," I said.

"It's a long drive," she said.

"Yup. But I've got my phone. I've got directions."

She was squinting at me, looking at me distantly, almost nostalgically, the way you'd look at a sunset. It was another humid, hot day, with everything slumping in the late-day haze. There was a charcoal smell from somewhere, and a tall redbrick building cast a long, lazy shadow across the street. Her eyes wandered over my shoulder. We stood there. She seemed to be wrestling with herself. Finally, she said, "I think it went well."

I felt a rush of relief, grateful she'd given me that. She looked, not happy exactly, but fortified.

"Yeah?" I said. "You do? I mean, I do, too. Your plates. It's obvious. People love them."

She smiled—she knew it, too. She adjusted the shoulder strap of her bag.

"Well," she said, and continued walking to her car.

I saw Elliot twice more before I left. Both times it was the same—I went to his apartment and he made dinner and we watched the screen for a while, searching for a signal, and then we had sex. It wasn't a whole lot different from the first time we did it, but I became more comfortable, more aware of what was going on. It was interesting, and involved, and companionable, and like going out of time for a little while. You could see how it could get better and better. You could see why someone would just want to do this thing, and not do anything else. I liked his lean body, and the way he'd prop himself up on his elbow when we were done, and we'd talk. But there was never any mention that we'd see each other after I left.

My last night there, in his bed, I stared at the cover of the same paperback, *The Afternoon Planet*. It had a sphere on it, and in that sphere was an entire city, and it was all imbued with hazy 1970s light.

"Keep it," he said. "Take it with you."

"I thought you said it wasn't any good."

"It got better," he said. "You can remember me by it." He took it and then opened the cover and pointed at something. "See."

It was a stamp. It read: "Please return to Elliot Grouse at 1117 Willowtree Road, Allentown, PA."

"It's from when I was a kid," he said. "But I still use it and write it in all my books. I like to think of my old house still getting these sci-fi paperbacks."

I closed it, and smiled, and kissed his shoulder.

Strangely, and unexpected to us both, Viv and I started writing e-mails back and forth after I was gone. It began when I got in touch about a pair of earrings I'd left there. She wrote back and said she'd found them one afternoon in the sunroom, which she was having remodeled. I pictured the whole thing getting bulldozed—the floor and the careworn pillows, the wooden coffee table, all of it being replaced by modern furniture and gleaming fixtures.

In our e-mails, we seemed to find a frankness and humor that we'd never been able to achieve in person. I found myself chatting to her about my day—the European history class I was taking at San Antonio Tech, how I'd gotten a part-time job as a swimming instructor at the gym to make some money, what it was like to be in my old room. She kept me updated on her friends and the little dramas that were happening at her office. I found myself looking forward to her e-mails. She was funny in her writing and had a flair for describing the things that people did, the strange policies she had to adjust to at work, sending it all up in a sharp, wry way.

She'd decided to pay someone to make her a proper website. She'd submitted her plates to more art shows and had even received an honorable mention at a Southern Folk Art Exhibit she'd gone to with one of her friends, and that was pretty good for someone with hardly any formal artistic background. She was even thinking of going to a workshop in Vermont. And there had been other interest, too, in selling her plates.

I wish I could say she'd met someone. That she'd finally had some throaty relationship where she came out of her shell, and discovered earthly pleasures and really explored them. Wouldn't that be nice? To think that life would just *be* that way? I'm not saying it still can't.

I remember sitting on the front porch on one of my last nights there. The front door was open and music was wafting outside. It was warm and spongy and I was barefoot, wearing a big shirt. It was a dark night. There was a thick plaid of insect sounds and every once in a while you could see the light from a car crawl by in the distance. Feel young, I kept telling myself. Just feel young. I was still only twenty-six. Generally, I still felt dogged with anxieties about the future—what I was going to do when I got back to Texas, if I was going to go back to school or not, what was going to happen with my parents. I kept thinking of that plaza at San Antonio Tech, with the spindly new trees, where my mom took her test. I pictured myself walking across the way, in the sun, wearing a backpack. And then, unexpectedly—a heavy bubble of happiness rose in me.

It's strange, but my instinct was to suppress it, because it somehow didn't seem fitting. Why would you do that? Why would you feel the need to push down a feeling of joy that kicked up from the world? Just go with it, I told myself, because you never know. The grain of it doesn't tell you anything about its volume.

Acknowledgments

Thank you, William Boggess—your faith in this meant the world to me. Thank you, Laura Perciasepe, for your genius edits, which made this book a much better version of itself. Thank you, Julie Barer, for your guidance. For your insight and encouragement, thank you to Alena Smith, Gina Welch, Matt White, Molly Minturn, Nell Boeschenstein, and Kelley Libby. Thank you to my family—Mom, Dad, Ben, Dan, Nicole, and Melanie—and thank you to the Brocks. Thank you to Jynne Martin, Liz Hohenadel, Margaret Delaney, Alex Guillen, and everyone at Riverhead. Most of all, thank you to Adam, my husband, for more than I could ever name.